He had got it wrong. Horribly, terribly, unforgivably wrong.

He had been so adamant about it, so stubborn. He had not listened to Gisele's protestations of innocence. She had begged and pleaded with him to believe in her but he had not.

She had cried.

She had screamed.

She had pummelled at his chest with tears pouring down her face and yet he had walked away. He had cut her ruthlessly from his life just days before they were to be married. He had cut all contact with her. He had sworn on his life he would never see or speak to her again.

And yet she had been innocent.

His gut clenched with guilt and shame. He had always prided himself on never making an error of judgement. He aimed for perfection in every area of his life. But this time he had got it wrong—horribly, terribly, unforgivably wrong.

THE OUTRAGEOUS SISTERS

The twin sisters everyone's *talking about!*

Separated by secrets…

Having grown up in different families, Gisele and
Sienna live lives that are worlds apart. Then a very
public revelation propels them into the world's eye…

Drawn together by scandal!

Now the sisters have found each other—
but are they at risk of losing their hearts to the two men
who are determined to peel back the layers of their
glittering façades?

This month Gisele will find out if she really is

DESERVING OF HIS DIAMONDS?

Look out for Sienna's story, coming soon
from Mills & Boon® Modern™ Romance!

DESERVING OF HIS DIAMONDS?

BY
MELANIE MILBURNE

First published in Great Britain 2012
by Mills & Boon, an imprint of Harlequin (UK) Limited.
Harlequin (UK) Limited, Eton House, 18-24 Paradise Road, Richmond, Surrey TW9 1SR

© Melanie Milburne 2012

ISBN: 978 0 263 22699 7

Harlequin (UK) policy is to use papers that are natural, renewable and recyclable products and made from wood grown in sustainable forests. The logging and manufacturing process conform to the legal environmental regulations of the country of origin.

Printed and bound in Great Britain
by CPI Antony Rowe, Chippenham, Wiltshire

From as soon as **Melanie Milburne** could pick up a pen, she knew she wanted to write. It was when she picked up her first Harlequin Mills and Boon novel at seventeen that she realised she wanted to write romance. Distracted for a few years by meeting and marrying her own handsome hero, surgeon husband Steve, and having two boys, plus completing a masters in education and becoming a nationally ranked athlete (masters swimming) she decided to write. Five submissions later she sold her first book and is now a multi-published bestselling, award-winning *USA TODAY* author. In 2008, she won the Australian Readers Association's most popular category/series romance, and in 2011 she won the prestigious Romance Writers of Australia R*BY award.

Melanie loves to hear from her readers via her website, www.melaniemilburne.com.au, or on Facebook at www.facebook.com/pages/Melanie-Milburne/351594482609.

Recent titles by the same author:

HIS POOR LITTLE RICH GIRL
THE WEDDING CHARADE
  (The Sabbatini Brothers)
SHOCK: ONE-NIGHT HEIR
  (The Sabbatini Brothers)
SCANDAL: UNCLAIMED LOVE-CHILD
  (The Sabbatini Brothers)

Did you know these are also available as eBooks?
Visit www.millsandboon.co.uk

To Carol Marinelli—
not just a fellow author
but also a fabulous and fun friend. XX

CHAPTER ONE

EMILIO was sitting in a café in Rome not far from his office when he finally found out the truth. His chest seized as he read the article about twin girls who had been separated at birth due to an illegal adoption. The article was journalism at its best: an intriguing and poignant account of how identical twins had finally been reunited, quite by chance, after a shop attendant mistook one for the other in a Sydney department store.

One mistaken for the other...

Emilio ignored his coffee and sat back in his chair and looked out at the bustling city crowds wandering past. Tourists and workers, young and old, married and single—everyone going about their business, totally unaware of the shock that was consuming him until he could scarcely breathe.

It hadn't been Gisele in the sex tape.

His throat felt as if a spanner were going down sideways. He had been so adamant about it, so stubborn. He had not listened to Gisele's protestations of innocence. He had *refused* to listen. She had begged and pleaded with him to believe in her, but he had not.

He had got it wrong.

She had cried. She had screamed. She had pummelled

at his chest with tears pouring down her face, and yet he had walked away. He had cut all contact with her. He had sworn on his life he would never see or speak to her again.

He had got it wrong.

Emilio's company had almost folded over the scandal. He'd had to work so hard to get back to where he was today. Eighteen-hour, sometimes twenty-four-hour days, sleepless nights, endless travel, jet lag so bad he didn't sleep properly any more, no matter how utterly exhausted he was. He went from project to project like an automaton, putting in the hours, signing up the deals, paying off the debts and then finally banking the millions, his drive to succeed knowing no bounds.

And for all this time he had blamed Gisele.

He had fuelled his hatred of her every day since. It had festered inside him like a gangrenous wound. He had felt it in every pore of his body. Every time he had thought of her the temperature of his wrath had risen. It had burned like a roaring furnace deep inside him. It had blazed like wild flames through his veins. Some days it had almost consumed him. It had been like a fever he could not control.

His gut clenched with a fist of guilt. He had always prided himself on never making an error of judgement. He aimed—some would say ruthlessly—for perfection in every area of his life. Failure was anathema to him.

And yet with Gisele he had got it wrong.

Emilio looked at his phone. He still had her number in his contacts. He had left it there as a reminder to trust no one, to let no one under his guard. He had never thought of himself as the sentimental type, but when he brought her details to the screen his fingers shook slightly as they hovered over her name. Somehow calling out of the blue to say sorry didn't seem the right way to handle things. He owed her a face-to-face apology. It was the least he could do. He wanted to erase that mistake, to draw a line through it and move on with his life.

He clicked on his phone's rapid dial instead and called his secretary. 'Carla, cancel all of my appointments for the next week and get me a flight to Sydney as soon as you can,' he said. 'I have some urgent business to see to there.'

Gisele was showing a first time mother the handmade christening gown she had embroidered when Emilio Andreoni came in. Seeing him standing there, so tall, so out of place in her baby clothes boutique made her heart leap to her throat like a gymnast on an overused trampoline.

She had practised this day over in her head just in case he took it upon himself to apologise once he found out about her long-lost identical twin. She had imagined how vindicated she would feel that he would have to admit he had got it wrong about her. She had imagined she would look at him and feel nothing, nothing but the bitter hatred of him for his cruel and ruthless rejection and his inexcusable lack of trust.

And yet that first glimpse of him sent a shockwave through her that made her feel as if the floor beneath her feet were suddenly shifting. Emotions she had bolted down with bitter determination suddenly popped against their restraints. One by one she could feel them spreading through her, making her chest ache with the weight of them. How could it physically hurt to see someone face to face? How could her heart feel pain like a stab wound at seeing his tall, imposing frame standing there? How could her insides clench and twist when his coal-black eyes met hers?

Gisele had seen him in the press several times since their break-up and although each time it had made her feel a tight sort of ache, it had felt nothing like the raw, claw-scraping pain of this.

He still had the same darkly tanned olive skin. The same Roman nose, the same penetrating dark brown eyes, the same intractable jaw that right now looked as if it hadn't seen a razor in the last thirty-six hours. The slightly wavy black hair was a little longer than the last time she had seen him—it was curling around the collar of his shirt and it looked as if his fingers had been the last thing that had moved through it. There were bruiselike shadows beneath his thickly lashed bloodshot eyes, no doubt put there by yet another sleepless night out with one of his one-night stand bimbo bedmates, she imagined.

'Excuse me…' she said to the young mother. 'I won't be a minute.'

Gisele walked over to where he was standing next to the premature baby clothes. He had one of his hands on a tiny vest that had a pink rosebud with little green leaves embroidered at the neck. The vest looked so tiny against his hand and it occurred to her then that Lily would have been too small for it when she had been born.

'Can I help you with something?' she asked with a brittle look.

Emilio's eyes meshed with hers, holding them captive. 'I think you know why I am here, Gisele,' he said in that deep, rich voice she had missed so much. It moved along her skin like a caress, settling at the base of her spine like a warm pool of slowly spreading honey.

Gisele had to fight hard to keep her emotions in check. This was not the time to show him she was still affected by him, even if it was only physically. She had to be strong, to show him he hadn't destroyed her life with his lack of trust. She had to show him she had moved on, that she was self-sufficient and successful. She had to show him he meant *nothing* to her now. She drew in a breath and lifted her chin, keeping her voice cool and composed. 'Of course.' She gave him an impersonal on-off movement of her lips that was nowhere near a smile. 'How could I forget? The two-for-one sale on all-in-one suits we have on at the moment. You can have blue, pink or yellow. I'm afraid we're all out of the white.'

His gaze never once wavered from hers; it was as dark and mesmerising as ever. 'Is there somewhere we could talk in private?' he asked.

Gisele straightened her shoulders. 'As you can see I have customers to see to,' she said, indicating with a waft of her hand the young woman browsing along the racks.

'Are you free for lunch?' he asked, still watching her steadily.

Gisele wondered if he was studying her for flaws. Could he see the way her once creamy skin had lost its glow? Could he see the shadows below and in her eyes that no amount of make-up could disguise? He had always prized perfection. Not just in his work but in every facet of his life. He would find her sadly lacking now, she thought, in spite of her name and reputation finally being cleared. 'I own and run this business,' she said with more than a hint of pride. 'I don't take a lunch break.'

Gisele saw his dark critical gaze sweep over the baby wear boutique she had bought a few weeks after he had cut her from his life just days before their wedding. Building it up from yet another struggling suburban retail outlet to the successful exclusive affair it was now had been the only thing that had got her through the heartbreak of the past two years.

Some well meaning friends, along with her mother, had suggested it would have been better to have sold the business as soon as she had been told Lily wasn't going to make it, but somehow, in her mind, holding on to the shop was a way to hold on to her fragile little daughter for just that little bit longer. She felt close to Lily here, surrounded by the handmade blankets and bonnets and booties she made for other babies to wear. It was her only connection now with motherhood and she wasn't going to relinquish it in spite of the pain it caused to see those brand-new prams being pushed through the door day after day. No one knew how hard it was for her to look and not touch those precious little bundles inside. No one knew how long at night she clung to the bunny blanket she had made for Lily's tiny body to be wrapped in during those few short hours of her life.

Emilio's eyes came back to connect with hers. 'Dinner then,' he said. 'You don't work past six, do you?'

Gisele watched in irritation as the young mother left

the shop, no doubt put off by Emilio's brooding presence. She sent him a glare. 'Dinner is out of the question,' she said. 'I have another engagement.'

'Are you involved with someone?' he asked, pinning her with his eyes.

She worked hard at keeping her composure. Did he really think she would have dived headfirst into another relationship after what he had done to her? She often wondered if she would ever feel safe in a relationship again. But she daren't admit to her singleton status. She had a feeling he wasn't just here to apologise and to clear the air between them. She could see it in the dark magnetic pull of his gaze. She could sense it in the atmosphere, the way the air she shared with him thickened with each breath she took into her lungs. Damn it, she could even feel it in her traitorous body as it reacted to his dark, disturbing presence the way it had always done in the past. Her senses went on full alert, her legs giving a little tremble as she thought of how he had taught her all she knew about physical intimacy, how it had been his body and his alone that had shown her what hers had been capable of in giving and receiving pleasure. 'I can't see how that is any of your business,' she said with a hoist of her chin.

A muscle flexed beside his mouth. 'I know this is hard for you, Gisele,' he said. 'It's hard for me too.'

'Meaning you never thought you'd ever have to apologise to me for getting it wrong?' she asked with a cutting look. 'Hate to say I told you so.'

His expression immediately became shuttered, closed off, remote. 'I'm not proud of how I ended things,' he

said. 'But you would have done the same if things were
the other way around.'

'You're wrong, Emilio,' she said. 'I would have looked
high and low for an alternative explanation for how that
tape came about.'

'For God's sake, Gisele,' he said roughly. 'Do you
think I didn't look for an explanation? You told me you
were an only child. *You* didn't even know you had a
twin. How was I supposed to come up with something
as bizarre as that? I looked at that tape and I saw you.
I saw the same silver-blonde hair, the same grey-blue
eyes, even the same mannerisms. I had no choice but to
believe what I was seeing.'

'You *did* have a choice,' Gisele said, shooting him a
blistering glare. 'You could have believed me in spite
of, not because of, the evidence. But you didn't love
me enough to trust me. You didn't love me at all. You
just wanted a perfect wife to hang off your arm. That
wretched tape tarnished me so I was of no further use
to you. It wouldn't have mattered if the truth had come
out in two minutes or two hours instead of two years.
Your business was always going to be the priority. You
put it before everything.'

'I put my business on hold to come out here to see
you,' he said, frowning at her broodingly.

'You've seen me, so now you can jump back on your
private jet and fly all the way back,' she said, sending
him a haughty look as she spun on her heel.

'Damn it, Gisele,' he said, snagging one of her arms
to stall her.

Gisele felt the steely grip of his long, strong fingers
on her bare arm as he turned her back to face him. His

touch was like a flame. It seared her skin like a brand. Every nerve flinched beneath her skin. She felt her stomach go hollow as his eyes locked on hers. She didn't want to lose herself in that glittering dark gaze. Not again. Once was enough. It had been her downfall, falling for a man with the inability to love and trust.

She didn't want him this close.

She could smell the heat of him, the sharp and heady cocktail of musk and male and lemon-based aftershave that made her nostrils flare and tingle. She could see the black pepper of the stubble on his jaw and her fingers suddenly itched to feel that sexy rasp under the soft pads of her fingertips. She could see the grim line of his beautifully sculptured mouth. The mouth that had wreaked such havoc on her senses from the very first time he had kissed her. She only had to close her eyes to remember how it felt to have those hard, insistent lips press down on hers…

She snapped out of her reverie like an elastic band that had been stretched too far. That same mouth had vilified her cruelly. Her ears still rang with his hateful, unforgettable, unforgivable words. There was no way she was going to let him off lightly, if at all. Her life had come undone the day he had cut her adrift. She had been so devastated and alone. Her happy future had suddenly been ripped away from her without warning. She had been shattered by his accusations. She had been left so raw with pain she had barely been able to drag herself through each agonising day.

Finding out she was pregnant a couple of months after she had returned to Sydney had been her only glimmer of hope in that very dark place she had found herself in.

But then that hope had been cruelly dashed a few weeks later at the second ultrasound. She had always wondered if that was her punishment for not telling Emilio about the pregnancy. He had forbidden all contact after their break-up, but she had been too devastated and hurt to even try.

And too angry.

She had wanted to punish him for not believing in her. She still wanted to punish him. It was like a rod of steel inside her. The only thing holding her upright was her fury and resentment and hatred towards him. Nothing was going to melt it.

'Why are you making this harder than it already is?' Emilio asked.

Gisele needed the trench of her anger to hide in and the deeper and dirtier the better. 'You think you can breeze in here and issue some half-hearted apology and I'll forgive you?' she asked. 'I'll *never* forgive you. Do you hear me? *Never.*'

The line of his mouth was grim. 'I don't expect you to forgive me,' he said. 'I do, however, expect you to act like an adult and hear me out.'

'I'll act like an adult when you stop restraining me like an out of control child,' she said, shooting him a livid look. 'Let go of my arm.'

His fingers softened their hold but he didn't release her. Gisele felt her heart give a nervous flutter as the broad pad of his thumb slid down to her pulse. Could he feel the thud of those hit-and-miss beats? She surreptitiously moistened her mouth but his gaze caught the movement. His eyes darkened, the pupils disappearing into the chocolate-brown of his irises. She knew that look so well. It triggered a visceral reaction in her body. The pulse of longing was like a lightning strike to that secret place between her thighs. Every erotically sensual moment they had ever shared flashed through her brain like a film on fast-forward. Those sensually provocative images made a mockery of every paltry attempt she had made to keep herself immune. What hope of immunity when one look from those dark eyes made her blood rush through her veins at breakneck speed?

'Have dinner with me tonight,' he said.

'I told you I already have an engagement,' she said, not quite meeting his eyes.

Emilio tipped up her chin with his other hand, his eyes dark and penetrating as they held hers. 'And I know you are lying,' he said.

'What a pity you weren't such a hotshot detective two years ago,' she threw back resentfully as she finally managed to break free. She stood and pointedly rubbed at her wrist, still glaring at him.

'I'll pick you up at seven,' he said. 'Where do you live?'

Gisele felt a bolt of panic rush through her. She didn't want him at her flat. That was her private sanctuary, the one place she felt safe enough to let out her grief. Besides, how would she explain all the photos of Lily? It was much better to leave him ignorant of their baby's short life. She wasn't ready to tell him. She would *never* be ready to tell him. How could she cope with the pain of him telling her she should have had a termination as she had been advised? It had been hard enough hearing it from her mother and some of her friends. Emilio wouldn't have wanted a child who wasn't perfect. It wouldn't have suited his plan for a perfectly ordered life.

'You don't seem to be getting the message, Emilio,' she said with a defiant look. 'I don't want to see you again. Not tonight. Not tomorrow night. Not ever. You've apologised. End of story. Now, please leave before I have you evicted by Security.'

His expression was faintly mocking. 'What Security?' he asked. 'Anyone could walk in here and empty your cash register while your back was turned and you wouldn't be able to do a single thing to stop them. You don't even have CCTV cameras installed.'

Gisele pressed her lips together, hating him for pointing out what he obviously perceived as a flaw in her personality. Her mother...*her adoptive mother*, she corrected herself, had communicated much the same thing only a few days ago, saying she was far too trusting with her customers. It didn't come naturally to Gisele to mistrust people, but then wasn't that why her life had ended up the way it had? She had been so naive and trusting with Emilio and it had backfired spectacularly.

Emilio continued to study her for a lengthy moment. 'Have you been ill recently?' he asked.

Gisele suddenly froze, caught off guard by that dark penetrating gaze that refused to let hers go. 'Um...why do you ask that?'

'You look pale and much thinner than when we were together,' he said.

'Not quite up to your impeccable standards any more?' she said, giving him a hardened look. 'What a lucky escape you had in calling off our wedding. It wouldn't suit your image to be married to a frump, now, would it?'

Another heavy frown appeared between his brows. 'You misunderstand me,' he said. 'I was simply commenting on your pallor, not your lack of beauty. You are still one of the most beautiful women I have ever seen.'

It was amazing how easily cynicism came to Gisele now. In the past she would have blushed and felt incredibly flattered by such a compliment. Now all she felt was a simmering fury that he was trying to charm her into forgiving him. He was wasting his time and hers. *Forgiveness* was a word she had long ago deleted from her vocabulary.

She walked over to the shop service counter and barricaded herself behind it. 'You can save your shallow compliments for someone who will believe them enough to fall into your bed,' she said. 'It's not going to work with me.'

'Is that why you think I am here?' he asked.

Gisele felt herself being swallowed by that charcoal-black unreadable gaze. The air seemed to be charged with an erotic energy she had no control over. Her hands gripped the edge of the counter for support, her heart beating too hard and too fast as his hooded gaze slipped to her mouth.

She held her breath in that infinitesimal moment as his gaze rested on her lips.

His gaze was like a touch. It burned her with its intent. She felt the tingle of her lips as if he had reached across the counter and pressed his mouth to hers…

But her best friend cynicism came to her rescue just in time. 'I think you are here to clear your conscience,' she said. 'You're not here because of me. You're here because of you.'

His expression gave no clue to what was going on behind the screen of his dark eyes, but a tiny nerve twitched at the edge of his mouth as if it were being tugged by an invisible needle and thread.

It seemed a very long time before he spoke.

'I am here for both of us,' he said. 'I want to wipe the slate clean. Neither of us can truly move on with our lives with this lying like a festering sore between us.'

Gisele put up her chin with cool hauteur. 'I *have* moved on with my life,' she said.

His eyes challenged hers for endless seconds, but when he finally spoke his voice was gruff. 'Have you, *cara*? Have you really?'

Was it his unexpectedly gentle tone or his use of an all too familiar endearment that made her throat suddenly close over as if someone had gripped it and cruelly squeezed? She blinked against the sting of tears, once, twice, three times before she was confident they were not going to break through. 'Of course,' she said coldly. 'Or would you rather I said I'd been pining for you forlornly ever since you cut me from your life?'

'That would indeed be a punishment I would not like to have inflicted on me,' he said with a rueful movement of his lips. 'It would make the guilt I feel all the harder to bear.'

Gisele looked at him standing there, so tall, so assured, the master of all he controlled. Was he really feeling guilty or just annoyed at being wrong for once in his life? He was a fiercely proud man. She had met no one prouder or more stubborn. 'You can sleep easy,

Emilio,' she said. 'After the way you treated me I put you out of my mind as soon as I stepped off the plane. I haven't thought of you in months.'

He held her look for a heartbeat longer than she would have liked. 'I'll be in town for the rest of the week,' he said, handing her a business card. 'If you change your mind about meeting with me, please feel free to call me at any time.'

Gisele took the silver-embossed card with a hand that trembled slightly as it came in contact with his. She curled her fingers around the card until its edges bit into her palm. 'I won't change my mind,' she said with steely determination wrapped around each and every word.

She waited until he had left before she let out her breath in a long ragged stream. She looked at the card she had crushed in her hand. A sharp corner had broken the skin of her palm; a very timely reminder that if she allowed Emilio Andreoni too close again she would be the only one to get hurt.

CHAPTER TWO

A couple of days later Gisele received a visit from her landlord, Keith Patterson. For a heart-stopping moment she wondered if she had somehow overlooked paying her rent, but then she remembered she had seen the electronic transfer of the funds on her accounts profile page only the week before.

'I know this is short notice, Miss Carter,' Keith said after the usual polite exchange of greetings, 'but I've decided to sell the building to a developer. I got an offer too good to refuse. The wife and I lost a fair bit in the global financial crisis and we need to refinance ourselves for our retirement. This offer couldn't have come at a better time.'

Gisele blinked at him in alarm. While her profit turnover was good and her bank overdraft manageable, finding other premises would no doubt involve a rise in rent. She didn't want to overstretch herself, especially as she had only recently employed an assistant. So many small businesses folded due to having too many overheads and not enough income. She didn't want to become another statistic of economic disaster. 'Does that mean I have to move out?' she asked.

'That will depend on the new owner,' Keith said.

'He'll have to get council approval before he does any alterations. That could take weeks or a couple of months. He gave me his card for you to contact him to discuss the lease.' He handed her a silver-embossed card across the counter.

Gisele's heart dropped like a stone inside her chest even before she saw the name on the card. 'Emilio Andreoni bought the building?' she asked in a shocked gasp.

'You've heard of him?' Keith asked.

She felt her face grow warm. 'Yes…I've heard of him,' she said. 'But he's an architect, not a property developer.'

'Maybe he's diversifying his interests,' Keith said. 'I've heard he's won numerous awards for his designs. He seemed mighty keen to buy the place.'

'Did he give you a reason for his enthusiasm?' Gisele asked, boiling with anger inside.

'Yes, he said it held sentimental value,' Keith said. 'Maybe a relative of his owned it in the past. Some Italians used to have a fruit shop here in the fifties. I can't remember their name.'

Gisele ground her teeth. Sentimental value indeed! She knew for a fact Emilio had no living relatives, or at least none he wanted to associate with. He had told her very little about his background, but she sensed it hadn't been much like hers. She had often wondered if that was another reason he had wanted to marry her. Her blue-blooded pedigree had appealed to him. How ironic that it turned out she and her twin were the products of an illicit affair their father had had with a housekeeper while he and his wife were living in London.

Once Keith Patterson had gone Gisele looked at the business card lying on the counter. She drummed her fingers on the glass surface, her teeth almost going to powder as she considered her options. She could tear up the card into tiny little pieces as she had a couple of days ago, or she could call the mobile number on it and arrange a showdown. If she tore up the card he would surely come in to see her and she would be caught off guard just as she had been before.

She decided it would be better to see him on her terms this time around. She picked up the phone and started dialling.

'Emilio Andreoni.'

'You bastard!' Gisele spat before she could stop herself.

She heard the sound of a leather chair squeaking as he shifted position. She imagined him with his feet up on the desk, his ankles crossed casually, his head laid back against the headrest and a self-satisfied smile on his mouth.

'Nice to hear from you, Gisele,' he said smoothly. 'Have you changed your mind yet about meeting with me one last time before I leave?'

Gisele almost broke the phone with the pressure of her fingers as she gripped it in her hand. 'I can't believe how ruthless you're prepared to be in getting your own way,' she hissed at him. 'Do you really think by charging me an exorbitant rent it will make me hate you less?'

'You're assuming I'm going to charge you rent,' he said. 'Maybe I'll lease the premises to you without charging a cent.'

Gisele's heart clanged against her rib cage. 'Wh-what did you say?'

'I'm offering you a business proposition,' he said. 'Meet with me and we'll discuss it.'

She felt a shiver of apprehension trickle down her spine like a single drop of icy water. 'I'd rather turn tricks on the nearest street corner than have anything to do with you,' she threw back.

'Before you reject an offer you really should discuss the terms and conditions more thoroughly,' he said. 'You might be surprised at some of the benefits.'

'I can just imagine some of the benefits,' Gisele said, her voice liberally laced with scorn. 'A rent-free premises in exchange for my body and my self-respect. No thanks.'

'You really should consider my proposal, Gisele,' he said. 'It wouldn't do to put at risk everything you've worked so hard for, now, would it?'

'I've lost everything before and survived,' she said, throwing a verbal punch.

She heard it land with a sharp intake of his breath. 'Don't make me play dirty, Gisele,' he gritted. 'I can and I will if I have to.'

Gisele felt that icy shiver again. She knew just how ruthless he could be. She knew he had ways and means to make things very difficult for her, even more difficult than when he had thrown her out of his life so callously just days before the wedding she had planned with such excitement and anticipation. She still remembered the horror of that moment. She couldn't even look at a wedding gown now without feeling that gut-wrenching sense of despair. But she was not going to roll over for him. 'I don't want or need your help,' she said. 'I don't care if I have to beg on the streets. I will not accept anything from you.'

'I recently designed a holiday retreat for one of Europe's largest retail giants,' Emilio said. 'With a click of a computer mouse I could make your business expand exponentially. Your shop will not just be a local enterprise. It will instantly become a global brand.'

Gisele thought of the expansion she had planned over the next few years. How she had imagined building her business to spread to other suburban outlets and to the larger department stores and, more importantly, increasing her online presence. The only things that had been holding her back were secure finance and the right contacts.

She fought with her resolve. She wanted to say no. She wanted to slam the phone down in his ear. But turning her back on him would mean turning her back on the sort of success most people could only dream about. But then, doing any sort of business deal with Emilio would mean contact with him.

Contact she didn't want, wouldn't *allow* herself to want.

Her stomach slipped like a cat's claws on a highly polished surface.

Maybe even intimate contact...

'Think about it, Gisele,' he said. 'You have a lot to gain by allowing me back in your life, even if it's only temporarily.'

'What do you mean, temporarily?' she asked warily.

'I would like you to spend the next month with me in Italy,' Emilio said. 'It will give us a chance to see if we can still make things work between us. I will, of course, pay you an allowance for the time we spend together.'

'I'm not spending the next minute with you,' Gisele said with a fresh upsurge of resolve. 'I'm hanging up right now so don't bother call—'

'It will also be the perfect opportunity for me to introduce you to the right contacts,' he said. 'How does a million dollars for the month sound?'

Gisele's mouth opened and closed. She couldn't seem to get her voice to work. Her heart was pumping so hard and so fast she felt as if it were going to explode out from between her breasts and land on the floor in front of her.

A million dollars.

Could she do it? Could she survive a month living with Emilio? She had shared his bed with love in the past. How could she do it this time with hatred?

Would he *want* her to share his bed?

A shiver ran over her skin. Of course he would want her to. Hadn't she seen his desire for her burning in his dark eyes when he came into the shop? Couldn't she hear the spine-tingling rumble of it in his voice now? 'I…I need some time to think about this,' she said.

'What's to think about?' he asked. 'You win either way, Gisele. If after a month we both feel there's no point in carrying on any further, you will be free to go. No strings. You can take the money and leave.'

She chewed at her bottom lip for a moment. 'And you're happy to have me back in your life, hating you the way I do?' she asked.

'I understand your feelings,' he said. 'But I feel we both need to be sure we're not making the biggest mistake of our lives by not exploring the possibility of a future together.'

Gisele frowned. 'Why are you doing this?' she asked. 'Why not leave things as they are?'

'Because as soon as I saw you the other day I knew we had unfinished business,' he said. 'I felt it and I know you did too. You can deny it but it won't make it any less real. You might hate me but I felt your body react to mine. You still want me just as much as I still want you.'

Gisele hated that he knew her body so well that he could read its most subtle of signals. What hope did she have of coming out of this with her pride intact? 'I want another day or two to think it over,' she said. 'And if I agree, I won't accept less than two million.'

'I can see why you have done so well for yourself in the time we've been apart,' Emilio said musingly. 'You drive a hard bargain. Two million is a lot of money.'

'I have a lot of hate,' she shot back.

'I will look forward to dismantling it,' he said.

Gisele felt her insides clench with unruly desire. 'You haven't got a hope, Emilio,' she said. 'You can pay all you like for my body but you will never have my heart.'

'Your body will do for now,' he said with smouldering intensity. 'I will send a car for you on Friday evening. Pack your passport and some clothes if it is a yes.' And with that the phone line went dead.

As Emilio's driver pulled up in front of her block of flats Gisele told herself she was saying yes for one reason and one reason only. She wanted to make Emilio's life as miserable as she could for the next month. She would enjoy every minute of making him regret the way he had treated her. He would not find her such an easy conquest this time around. She was not the sweet, shy, rather naive virgin he had met and swept off her feet two years ago. She was older and wiser, harder and more cynical. More battle scarred and dangerously, scarily angry.

Also, being in Europe for a month might give her the opportunity to get to know the sister she had never met until a couple of weeks ago. Sienna was currently living in London, which was a whole lot closer to Rome than Sydney.

Gisele felt her chest tighten as she thought of all the lost years, all the lost confidences and closeness she and Sienna should have had together. Selfish adults who had not stopped to think of the long-term consequences of such a reckless and self-serving deception had stolen it from them.

She was still coming to terms with the heartbreak of finding out the truth. It wasn't just about the sex tape scandal mix-up, although that was heartbreaking enough. She felt her whole life had been a lie. She didn't know who she was any more. It was as if Gisele Carter, the Sydney born and bred only child of Richard and Hilary Carter, had suddenly vanished, vaporised into thin air.

Who was she now?

She was not her mother's daughter. And yet she was not her biological mother's daughter either as she had never felt her mother's arms or ever felt the brush of her lips on her skin, or if she had in those first early days after birth she had no memory of it now.

She had been handed over like a package, a one-way delivery, never to be returned to sender. How had her mother, Nell Baker, chosen which baby to keep and which one to give away? Had she done it willingly or had she done it for the money?

A little dagger of guilt pierced Gisele as she thought of what she had led Emilio to believe *she* would do for money. He thought he could pay any amount to have her back in his life and back in his bed but he was in for a big surprise. She gave a grimly determined smile as she pressed down on the suitcase to snap the locks closed. Once the month was up Emilio would be just as glad to see the back of her as he had been the last time.

She would make sure of it.

Emilio was waiting in the hotel bar when Gisele came. He felt the jolt of awareness hit him like a punch to his abdomen. He had met hundreds of beautiful women but no one had that powerful physical effect on him just by walking into the room. And yet she hardly seemed to be aware of how every male head turned and looked at her.

Her simple but elegant cream dress was nipped in at the waist with a black bow at the front that drew attention to how slim she was. He suspected he could now span her waist with his hands. Her silver-blonde hair was pulled back in a smooth knot at the back of her head, showcasing the swanlike grace of her neck. She was wearing make-up but it was so skilfully applied it looked entirely natural. She had subtly highlighted the grey-blue of her eyes with eyeliner and a brush of smoky eyeshadow, and her lush lips were shiny with pink-tinted lipgloss. It made him want to lean down and press his lips to hers to see if she still tasted the same. He could smell her perfume, her signature summery honeysuckle scent that had clung to his skin for hours after making love with her. He had missed that fragrance. It never smelled quite the same on anyone else.

He stood to greet her, and even though she was wearing shiny patent black killer heels he still towered over her. 'Did you bring your passport?' he asked.

She gave him a churlish look from beneath her lashes. 'I almost didn't, but the thought of two million reasons why I should made me see reason.'

Emilio allowed himself a small smile of satisfaction. She was here under duress but at least she was here. He led her to a quiet corner in the bar with a gentle hand at her elbow. He felt her bare skin shiver in response to his touch and an arrow of need staked him in his groin. Her skin was so soft and creamy, like silk against his fingers. 'What would you like to drink?' he asked. 'Champagne?'

She shook her head. 'I'm not celebrating anything,' she said, shooting him another look. 'White wine will do.'

Emilio ordered their drinks and, once they had been served, he leaned back in his seat to study her ice-maiden features. He knew he deserved her ire. He had thrown her out of his life with a callous and ruthless disregard for her feelings. He had been so convinced she had betrayed him. The red mist of anger he had felt had blinded him to anything but what he believed she had done. The image of her with that man taunted him and had done so until he had found out about the discovery of her identical twin.

Seeing her in the flesh again had brought back all the

reasons he had wanted to marry her in the first place. It wasn't just her natural beauty or grace or poise. It wasn't just her softly spoken voice and the way she nibbled at her bottom lip when she was feeling uncertain, or the way she sometimes twirled a loose strand of hair around one of her fingers when she was concentrating on something. It was something in her eyes, those incredible were-they-grey-were-they-blue eyes that had warmed and softened the first time she'd looked at him. What man didn't want the woman he had chosen to be his wife to look at him like that?

As far as he had been concerned, Gisele had been perfect wife material, sweet and gentle, biddable and loving. The fact that he hadn't been in love with her was irrelevant. For his whole life love had been an emotion he had never been able to rely on. In his experience, people used the words so freely but their actions rarely backed them up. The sex tape scandal had reinforced to him how pointless it was to love someone, for people *always* let you down. But in the end he had been the one to let *her* down. He had destroyed her love with his lack of trust in her. But he was determined to get her back. He would make it up to her in a thousand different ways. He couldn't allow a failure like this to blot his life. It felt like a giant ink stain on his soul. He had made the error and it was up to him to do whatever it took to fix it.

And he would do *whatever* it took.

He knew she still wanted him. He had seen it that first day in her shop, the way her body spoke to him in its own private language. His own intensely visceral response to her had sideswiped him. He had thought he had put his desire for her behind him, but it was back with a vengeance as soon as he had laid eyes on her. It was an aching, pulsing need to feel her in his arms again. He couldn't wait to take her upstairs and prove to her they still had a future, that the past could be permanently put aside, erased as if it hadn't happened. She was playing coy with him but he was sure once he kissed her she would melt, just as she always had in the past. He could not tolerate any other outcome.

Failure was not an option.

'I have arranged a flight for tomorrow,' he said. 'We leave at 10:00 a.m.'

Gisele gave him a brittle look. 'You were that certain I'd come?'

He returned her look with measured calm. 'Let's say I know you well enough to be quietly confident,' he said.

'You don't know me any more, Emilio,' she said with another hardened look. 'I'm not the same person I was two years ago.'

'I don't believe that,' Emilio said. 'I know we all change a bit over time but you can't really change who you are deep inside.'

She lifted a slim shoulder in a devil-may-care manner. 'Maybe in a month you'll change your mind,' she said and took a sip of her drink.

'Is your sister still here in Sydney?' Emilio asked.

'No, she flew back to London ten days ago,' she said, looking into the contents of her glass with a little frown. 'The press were hounding her. They were hounding us both. I found it a little scary...' She bit her lip and drained her glass as if she wanted to stop any more words coming out of her mouth.

'It must have been a very difficult time for you both,' he said.

She lifted her gaze to his; her eyes were like stormy grey-blue ice cubes, hard, cold and resentful. 'I'd rather not talk about it if you don't mind,' she said. 'I'm still trying to sort it out in my head. So is Sienna.'

'Perhaps you can invite her to stay at my villa for a few days,' Emilio said. 'I would like to meet her.'

She gave another shrug of indifference. 'Whatever.'

Emilio signalled for the waiter to refresh their drinks. He sat back in his seat and observed Gisele as she tucked an imaginary strand of hair behind her ear, another one of her I'm-out-of-my-depth-and-trying-not-to-show-it mannerisms. She was not as immune to him as she tried to make out. He had seen the flare of female interest in her gaze. He had felt the shiver of reaction on her skin when he had touched her. One kiss would prove he could have her back where he wanted her.

'Tell me about your shop,' he said. 'How did you come about buying the business?'

She dropped her gaze to the drink the waiter had just set before her. 'When I came back…from Italy I…I wanted a secure base,' she said. 'I liked the idea of working for myself. Having more control, that sort of thing. I'd sold some items to the owner in the past and she gave me the first option of buying.'

'It's a big commitment for a young woman of just twenty-five, or twenty-three as you were then,' Emilio said. 'Did your parents help you?'

Gisele put her glass down. 'At first, but then things got a bit tricky after my father got sick. He had a few debts we didn't know about until after he'd died. Bad business decisions, a bit of gambling with the stock market that didn't pay off as well as he'd hoped. I had to help my mother…I mean Hilary out.'

Emilio put his drink down on the coaster on the table between them. 'I'm sorry I didn't send a card,' he said. 'I'd heard he was terminally ill. I should have made contact to offer my condolences. It must have been a very difficult time for you and your mother.'

She looked back at the contents of her glass; the grip of her fingers was so tight around the stem he wondered if it would snap. 'He took eight and a half miserable months to die,' she said. 'Not once in all that time did he ever say anything about me having a twin sister.' She looked at him at that point, her grey-blue gaze blazing with anger. 'Both my parents knew our relationship had broken up because of that sex tape but still neither he nor my mother said a word. I can never forgive them for that.'

Emilio carefully removed the wineglass from her stiff fingers and put it to one side. 'I can understand your anger towards them but our relationship broke up because I didn't trust you,' he said. 'If anyone is to blame it is me.'

Gisele met his gaze in the long silence that ensued. 'You know what really upsets me?' she asked.

'Tell me,' he said, still holding her gaze.

'How did they choose?' she asked.

'You mean who got which twin?' he asked.

Gisele blew out a hissing breath. 'I can't get it out of my mind,' she said. 'How did they do it? How could my mother, my biological mother, give me up? And how could my father ask it of her? And not only that, what was my adoptive mother thinking by agreeing to bring up her husband's love child? Did she have no self-respect?'

Emilio bent his forearms on his thighs so he could reach Gisele's tightly knotted hands. He took them both in one of his, stroking the tension away as best he could. 'Have you asked her about it?' he said.

She looked at him with flashing eyes. 'Of course I've asked her,' she said. 'She said she did it to keep my father happy. She spent their whole married life trying to make him happy but it never worked.'

'From what you told me, your family always seemed so perfect to me,' Emilio said, still stroking her hands. 'You never said anything about them being unhappy together.'

Gisele looked down at their joined hands and hastily pulled hers away. She sat straighter in her seat, ramrod straight, angry straight, keep-away-from-me straight. 'I never liked admitting it to anyone but I always felt I wasn't good enough for either of my parents,' she said. 'I tried my best but nothing I did or achieved seemed to please them. My mother wasn't the maternal type. She never liked cuddling me or playing with me. She employed a nanny to do that. Now I understand why. I wasn't her child.' She drew in another painful-sounding breath and continued, 'My father was just as bad. Deep down, I think he really wanted a son. My mother certainly couldn't give him one, but then his mistress gave him two daughters so he chose one. But I've often wondered if he thought he'd chosen the wrong one or whether he wished he had just walked away from both of us. He was stuck in a loveless marriage until the day he died, out of guilt presumably. All of those long stone-walling silences between him and my mother over the years suddenly made a whole lot of sense.'

Emilio frowned. He had never heard Gisele talk so honestly about her childhood. He had thought she had come from a reasonably happy and stable home. He had envied her background, given the bleak misery of his. It made him realise how little he had known her, even though he'd been days off marrying her. He had been struck by her beauty but had given little thought to who she was, what she valued and how she wanted her life to run. He had swept her off her feet, dazzled her with his wealth and charm, and yet had not known for a moment how deeply insecure she really was. It was like looking at her for the first time. The same beauty was there but so too was a fragility that he had not seen the first time around. But then she had been devastatingly hurt and he, to his shame, had done that to her, even more so than her parents. He wasn't sure how he could ever fix that terrible mistake but he was determined to try. 'How is your sister dealing with this?' he asked.

Gisele let her stiff shoulders drop. 'She's a lot more chilled about it than me,' she said. 'I guess growing up with a single mother who was known to be a bit of a tearaway has toughened her up rather a lot. It sounded like Sienna was the parent rather than the child most of the time. She told me there were always a lot of men coming and going in her mother's life. It can't have been an easy childhood but she just made the best of it.'

'Is she disappointed she didn't get to meet your father?'

'Yes and no, I suppose,' Gisele said, frowning a little. 'I think she would've given him a serve for what he did. She's a bit of a straight shooter. I think I could do with some lessons from her, actually. It's about time I learned to speak up for myself.'

'I think you're doing rather a good job of it,' Emilio said with a crooked smile. 'Perhaps I am wrong after all. Maybe you have changed.'

Her eyes glittered as they held his. 'You'd better believe it.'

Emilio allowed a little silence to pass before he spoke. 'Did you give the keys and all the relevant paperwork for your shop to the driver?'

'Yes.'

'Good,' he said. 'Your new assistant will hold the fort until you decide what course of action to take. I've already spoken to her about it.'

She frowned at him. 'What do you mean?'

He held her look for a moment. 'You might decide to stay on in Italy,' he said. 'It would be imprudent not to prepare for that possibility.'

She gave him a disdainful look. 'You must get really exhausted carrying that monumental ego around. Do you really think I will step back into your life as if nothing has changed? You're paying for a month and that's all you're going to get.'

Emilio fought back his temper. He was not used to her being so obstructive and defiant. In the past she had been so willing to fit in with his plans. Where was the sweet young woman he had chosen as his bride?

'Would you like another drink?' he asked after a tense pause.

'No… Thank you.' She pushed the glass away with another little frown pulling at her brow.

'I thought we could have dinner in my suite,' he said.

She looked at him with startled eyes. 'Why not in a restaurant?' she asked.

'I thought it might be more private.'

Her eyes narrowed. 'You can quit it with the whole seduction routine, Emilio,' she said. 'It won't work.'

Emilio felt his groin tighten as she threw the challenge down with her flashing gaze. 'You think not?' he asked.

'I know not,' she said with a lift of her chin.

He held her gaze, hot, hungry desire leaping like flames in his body. This new feisty Gisele was turning him on. There was something about her newfound defiance that thrilled him. It stirred his blood, making it surge through his system like rocket fuel. There was one thing he loved more than anything and that was a challenge. He had left his dirt-poor background behind with the same gritty determination to succeed no matter what it cost. He had put himself through school and then university, working day and night to cover the expense. He had made his fortune by rising to the demands of difficult clients and completing next to impossible projects. He had nearly lost it all after the scandal, but he had clawed his way back.

Gisele was another next to impossible project but, just like all the rest, he was determined to succeed.

Nothing and no one was going to stand in his way.

CHAPTER THREE

GISELE stood like a statue of marble as Emilio escorted her up to his suite. She could smell his aftershave; it stirred deep memories she tried desperately to suppress. She felt as if she were stepping back in time. How many times had she stepped into an elevator to accompany him up to his penthouse suite in hotels all over Europe? The erotic images that thought triggered made her skin prickle all over and she had to bite her lip until it hurt to block them from her mind.

Back then she had been so eager to please him. She knew right from the moment she had met him that he was a proud and strong-willed man but she had never questioned him, never stood up to him and never challenged him. She had just loved him, completely and desperately. How had she allowed herself to become so vulnerable? The power balance of their relationship had been wrong. She had loved him too much and he hadn't loved her at all.

It was only his pride that wanted her back now. She knew it wasn't about her as a person. He wanted the world to know he was setting the record straight. His offer of a one-month trial seemed to prove it. A man with his high profile could not afford to be seen as acting unfairly. The press had gone wild with the story of Sienna and her being reunited. She was surprised he hadn't already informed the media of his intention to resume his relationship with her.

The elevator stopped and Emilio held the doors back for her with an outstretched arm. Gisele moved past him, determined not to show how unsettled she was. Her stomach was twitching with nerves. Everything about him unsettled her. He seemed to see much more than she wanted him to see. What if he sensed she was hiding something from him? How long before he guessed the pain in her eyes had been put there, not just by him, but also by the loss of their child? The child whose soft pink bunny blanket that still held a faint trace of her sweet baby smell was folded inside her suitcase? She hadn't been able to leave that final link with Lily behind. Her mother...*Hilary*, she quickly amended, had said it was unhealthy to keep holding on. She had said Gisele should put it all behind her, pack the blanket away so she could finally move on.

Gisele wasn't ready to move on.

She didn't think she would ever be ready to move on. What would Hilary know anyway? She hadn't physically given birth to a child only to have that child's life snatched away. She didn't know, *couldn't* possibly know what it felt like...

'Relax, *cara*,' Emilio said as he opened the door to his suite. 'You look like you're about to be devoured by a wild beast.'

Gisele stalked past him. 'I have a headache,' she said and it wasn't a lie. The pain behind her eyeballs had gone from a dull ache to a pounding that felt as if a team of jackhammers on steroids had taken up residence inside her skull.

His brows moved together. 'Why didn't you say something earlier?' he asked.

'I'll be fine,' she said, licking her lips to give them some much-needed moisture. 'I probably shouldn't have had that second drink. I don't have a good head for alcohol.'

'When was the last time you ate?' he asked.

The fact that she had to think about it didn't go unnoticed by him, Gisele thought as she saw that dark frown deepen across his brow. 'I can't remember,' she said. 'It wasn't a priority. I had to get things sorted at my flat and at the shop.' She threw him a resentful scowl. 'You didn't give me much time.'

'I'm sorry but I have to get back to Rome for a project I'm working on,' he said. 'The client is a big one. I had to work hard to get the contract. It's worth several million.'

Gisele thought of all the money he earned from his designs. She suspected he hadn't come by it easily. He was a prime example of the adage that anyone could do anything if they had enough determination. And the one thing Emilio had in spades was determination. She could see it in the glittering depths of his dark eyes and the strong lines of his jaw, both hinting at the implacability of his nature. In the days and weeks ahead she would be going head to head with that intransigent personality. Who would eventually come out on top? She gave a little involuntary shiver. It was a nerve-jangling thought.

'I'll have dinner sent up immediately,' he said. 'The porter brought up your things earlier,' he said. 'Would you like me to get a housemaid to unpack it for you? I should have thought of it before.'

'No,' Gisele said, perhaps a little too quickly. She saw his eyebrows lift. *Yes, definitely too quickly.* 'We're… um…leaving tomorrow, in any case.'

He held her gaze for an infinitesimal moment. 'Would you prefer the guest suite tonight?' he asked.

Gisele gave him a flinty look. 'Where else did you expect me to sleep?'

He came up close and brushed her hot cheek with the backs of his bent knuckles. 'Do you really think you'll be sleeping in the spare room for the entire month?' he asked.

She brushed his hand away as if it were an annoying fly. 'I haven't signed anything that requires me to sleep with you.'

'That reminds me.' He moved away from her and opened a briefcase that was lying on a table near the window. He took out a document and brought it over. 'You should read it before you sign it,' he said, his expression now inscrutable. 'The full amount we agreed on will be transferred to your account on the completion of your stay.'

Gisele looked at the sheaf of papers, wishing she could walk away. But two million dollars was not the sort of money she could turn her back on right now. She took pride in her success so far; it had helped her cope. How much better would she feel if her baby wear became even more successful? What else did she have in her life other than her shop? It wasn't as if she was ever going to get married and have a family now. That dream was long gone.

She took the papers and sank to the nearest chair, casting her eyes over the words printed there. She read it in detail but it was as straightforward as he had said. After the month was up she would be two million dollars richer and would owe him nothing. She signed it with a hand that wasn't quite steady. 'There,' she said, shoving the papers at his chest.

He put them to one side before he faced her again. 'So, it looks like we have a deal.'

She lifted her chin. 'Yes,' she said. 'You just signed away two million dollars.' *For nothing.*

His lips moved up in a curl that had a hint of mockery about it. 'How long do you think you will hold out, mmm? A week? Two?'

She glared at him fiercely. 'If you want a bedmate then you'll have to look elsewhere. I'm not interested.'

'You're planning your own little payback, aren't you?' he asked, still with that sardonic half smile.

Gisele felt a betraying flush stain her cheeks. 'I don't know what you're talking about,' she said.

'You think I don't know how your mind works?' he asked. 'You plan to make me suffer every minute of the time we spend together. But do you really think that by snipping and snarling at me it will make me want you less? Don't fool yourself, Gisele. You will sleep with me again, not because I paid you, but because you just can't help yourself.'

Gisele thought she couldn't hate him more than at that moment. She wanted to slap his arrogant face for assuming she had no self-control, no discipline and no self-respect. 'I hate you with every cell in my body,' she snarled at him like a cornered cat, all claws and bared teeth. 'Do you realise that? I *hate* you.'

Emilio's calmness riled her even further. 'The fact that you feel something for me is good,' he said. 'I can handle anger. It is far better than cold indifference.'

Gisele was determined she would show him just how cold and indifferent she could be. 'OK then.' She kicked off her heels and began to unzip her dress. 'You want me to sleep with you? Then let's get it out of the way right here and now.'

He stood there watching her silently, hardly a muscle moving, apart from his eyes. She saw the flare of his pupils, the primal signal of male attraction as she stepped out of her dress, leaving it in a puddle of fabric on the floor. She was standing in just her bra and knickers before him. She had stood in a whole lot less before him two years ago. But suddenly she felt naked in a way she had never felt before. A shiver broke out over her skin and her stomach curdled at the thought of going any further with this.

She put her hands behind her back to unhook her bra but her fingers were suddenly fumbling and useless. She felt as if she was going to cry. The emotions were like a fountain inside her that had been blocked. The pressure was building and building. She could feel it behind her eyes; she could feel it inside her chest, a tight ache that burned like fire.

'Get dressed,' Emilio said curtly as he turned away.

Gisele felt as if he had ripped the ankle-deep carpet out from under her feet. She had been prepared to play him at his own game but he had somehow turned the tables on her. He wanted her but on his terms, not hers.

She felt foolish.

She felt uncertain.

She felt *rejected*.

She watched as he walked over to the bar and poured himself a drink. He tipped back his head and drained his glass and then set in down on the bar with a thump. His shoulders looked tense; the muscles were bunched beneath the fine cotton of his shirt. She remembered how those muscles felt under the soft pads of her fingertips, how she used to massage away those tight knots, how she used to press her mouth to that hot, salty male skin…

Gisele ran the tip of her tongue over her bone-dry lips. 'So,' she said, summoning up what was left of her paltry attempt at cold indifference, 'I take it you no longer require my services this evening?'

Emilio turned to look at her but his expression was difficult to read. 'I will have a meal sent up to you presently,' he said. 'Please make yourself at home. I'm going out.'

'Where are you going?' The question was out before she could stop it and, to her shame, it sounded scarily close to one a jealous wife might have asked.

He turned from the door and raked her with his cold indifferent gaze. 'Don't wait up,' he said and then he was gone.

Gisele picked up one of her shoes and threw it at the door, angry tears spilling from her eyes. 'Damn you,' she said. 'Damn you to hell.'

Emilio entered the penthouse at two in the morning. He had walked the streets of Sydney for hours, determined not to return until Gisele was safely out of his range. His body had ached to take what she was offering so defiantly but he was not going to give her any more reasons to hate him. He would bide his time, waiting for her to come to him, as he knew she would. One night would not be enough for either of them. He was counting on that. He knew as soon as she gave in to the sexual chemistry that sizzled between them she would want more. She was bitter and angry but he knew she would get over it. Time was a great healer and a month was surely long enough to see if what they had shared together before could be resurrected.

The meal he had sent up to the suite looked as if it had been barely touched. He frowned as he looked at the selection of dishes and the undrunk wine sitting on the dining table. Her lack of appetite could have been because of her headache, but he suspected it was more to do with her current I'll-show-you attitude.

He admired her for standing up to him. Not many people did. He had learned on the filthy backstreets of Rome how to intimidate people. Those skills had come in handy in his professional life. What he said went. People didn't argue with him. They didn't challenge or defy him. The women in his life—and there had been plenty—never argued with him. They played by his rules. He always made sure of that. And Gisele had been no different during their time together. She had been biddable and gracious, the perfect companion, the perfect hostess, the perfect woman to be his wife.

Emilio frowned as he wandered over to the windows to look at the harbour view below. Some would say he had selected a trophy wife but he had never thought of Gisele like that. He had genuinely liked having her around. She had been easy company, at ease with him and with others. He was proud to have her on his arm. She moved with such poise and grace, with such natural elegance.

He let out a sigh that pulled on something deep inside his chest. If it hadn't been for the scandal they would have celebrated their second wedding anniversary a couple of weeks ago. Perhaps they might have even had a child by now. They had talked about it. That was another of the reasons he had wanted her as his wife. She had been keen to have a large family, having grown up as an only child. And he had been just as keen. All those years in and out of ill-run foster homes or begging on the streets had made him envious of all those warm, well-lit homes he had wandered past, with their close-knit family units inside.

His envy of other people's homes had been his primary motivation to become an architect. He had been barely ten years old when he had made the decision. He had thought by designing hundreds of dream homes that he would be satisfied, but it hadn't had the effect he'd imagined. He suspected that having his own family would be the only thing that would truly satisfy him. That and that alone would be able to soothe the raw sore of loneliness that constantly oozed deep inside his soul.

He felt it now, the never-ending sense of something missing from his life, of being incomplete. Was that why he had been drawn to Gisele, because of her own previously unspoken of loneliness?

Emilio turned from the window when he heard a

sound behind him. 'You didn't eat your dinner,' he said, just as Gisele was searching for the light switch.

She put a hand up to her throat, her eyes wide with shock. 'I didn't see you there,' she gasped. 'You scared me half to death. Why didn't you put the lights on?'

'Maybe I prefer the dark.'

She clutched the edges of her wrap together close to her chest. 'You could have said something,' she said with an accusing glare.

'I did,' he said. 'I said you didn't eat your dinner.'

She gave him a testy look. 'Maybe I wasn't hungry.'

'You need to eat,' he said. 'You're too thin.'

'You need to keep your opinions to yourself,' she shot back.

Emilio came over to where she was standing. 'Weren't you able to sleep?' he asked.

She flicked some hair back off her face and gave him a defiant stare. 'What's it to you?'

'I'm concerned about you,' he said. 'You look like you haven't slept properly in months.'

'Concerned, are you?' She flashed her eyes at him like blue lightning. 'What a pity you weren't so concerned about my welfare when you tossed me out on the street two years ago.'

Emilio ground his teeth together to stop himself saying something he might regret later. He had always prided himself on his self-control but Gisele's stubborn refusal to meet him halfway was testing his limits. How long was she going to persist with this game of payback? He had made amends. Wasn't it time to move on? 'Would you like me to make you a hot milk drink?' he asked.

She gave a choked bubble of laughter that sounded almost hysterical. 'Yeah, why not?' she said. 'Maybe put a shot of whisky in it for good measure. Two shots. That should knock me out.'

Emilio poured milk into a mug and placed it in the microwave set near the bar. He leant back against the counter as he studied her. 'I know from experience that running a business, even a successful one, is stressful,' he said. 'I've had plenty of sleepless nights myself.'

She curled her lip at him. 'I'm sure you've found plenty of women to distract you from your spreadsheets.'

'Not as many as you might think,' he said.

She gave him a cynical look. 'Well, just for the record, I'm not opening my legs like one of your cheap gold-digging whores.'

'You didn't seem to have any problem with it in the past,' he said. 'And at a cool two million, *cara*, you are certainly not cheap.'

Gisele raised a hand to slap him but he intercepted it, holding her slim wrist with the steel handcuffs of his fingers. 'Don't even think about it,' he warned. 'You might not like the consequences.'

She fought against his hold, clawing at him, but it was like a kitten trying to fight off a panther. He was too strong. He was too close. He was too everything.

'What consequences?' she asked. 'What are you going to do? Hit me right back? Is that what rough, tough Italian guys do?'

His expression tightened. 'I would never lay a finger on you and you damn well know it.'

She gave him a challenging glare. 'You've got five fingers on me right now.'

'And they're staying on you until you stop behaving like a wilful child.'

'I hate you,' she spat at him furiously.

'So you've said.'

'I mean it.'

'I believe you.'

'I want you to die and rot in hell.'

'I believe that too,' he said. 'But trading insults isn't going to make this go away.'

Gisele felt his thighs way too close to hers. She felt the warmth of his body, a radiating heat that her colder flesh craved. She felt his warm brandy-scented breath move like a teasing feather over her face. She felt her breasts go to hard aching peaks as the hard wall of his muscular chest loomed closer. Her lashes lowered as she looked at the line of his mouth. That mouth had kissed her so many times she had lost count. It could be hard and yet so soft, so demanding and yet so giving. 'I hate you,' she said again, but she wasn't sure if she was saying it for herself or for him.

She *needed* her anger.

She needed her rage and fury to keep herself in one piece. It was all she had. The only armour left that she could rely on. It had carried her through for so long.

Emilio cupped the side of her face with the broad span of his hand, his thumb moving over the hollow of her cheek, back and forth in a mesmerising rhythm that sent every thought flying out of her head. His eyes moved over her face, taking their time before they finally meshed with hers. 'Stop fighting me, Gisele,' he said. 'Don't give up on us before we've had a chance to set things right.'

'Some things can't be fixed,' she said. 'It's too late. Too much time has passed.'

'Do you really believe that?' he asked.

Gisele didn't know what to believe when he was holding her against him, his hard body fitting against her softer one as if no time had passed at all. She felt the hardened ridge of him, the surge of blood that lengthened him in the primal preparation to mate. It was so earthy and real. No amount of denying it could make it go away. Her body was responding to him in its own secret way. The silky moisture of her inner core was reminding her that she was no less immune to him than she had ever been. It didn't matter how much she hated him. It didn't matter how much she told him she wanted nothing more to do with him. Her body had its own needs and wants and they were overriding every other rational thought she tried to cling to.

'I believe you're only doing this because you're worried what the press and your precious business colleagues will think if you don't try to make amends,' she said, looking at him defiantly. 'It's all for show. The one-month reconciliation. You'll appear to do the right thing by me but it will all be for nothing because I won't come back to you for good. No amount of money will ever induce me to do that.'

He pulled her roughly up against him, his expression hard and bitter and thunderously angry. 'Then I'd better get my money's worth while I can, hadn't I?' And then his mouth crashed down on hers.

It was a blistering kiss, no hint of softness about it. Gisele felt its impact from the top of her prickling scalp to her toes curling into the carpet at her feet for purchase. His lips ground against hers with bruising force, making a dam inside her break its bounds. She kissed him back with all the fury that was inside her. She felt the demand of his tongue at the seam of her mouth and didn't hesitate in allowing him in.

She *wanted* him in.

She wanted to duel with him until they were both breathless with need. She wanted to taste him, to savour that essential maleness that had always sent ripples of delight through her body.

She wanted to hurt him. She wanted to remind him of what he had thrown away. She used her teeth, and not just little nippy bites either. She bit down on his lower lip and held on like a tigress with a prized piece of prey.

He bit her back, the alpha-male-taming-his-mate action sending a rapid blast of heat straight to her core. She tasted blood and wasn't sure if it was his or her own. She felt the rough graze of his stubbly jaw against her face as he changed position. His hands were clutching her head, his fingers buried deep in her hair, holding her captive to his sensual assault.

Gisele's hands moved up from lying flat against his chest to rediscovering the thick silkiness of his hair. He shifted against her urgently, his body so thick and full she felt her body quiver in reaction. Raw need clawed at her, an ache that was so tight and ravenous it burned inside her.

She wanted him.

She wanted him even though she hated him. She wanted the savage thrust of his possession to make her feel alive again. Oh, dear God, please make her feel *alive* again…

Emilio suddenly pulled away from her, his hands dropping from her as if she were a carrier of some deadly disease. He wiped at his mouth with the back of his hand, grimacing as he saw a smear of blood. 'Is that yours or mine?' he asked.

'Does it matter?' Gisele asked with an arch look.

'Actually it does,' he said, frowning darkly. 'I didn't intend to hurt you.'

She challenged him with her gaze as she touched a finger to where her bottom lip had borne the brunt of his kiss. 'Didn't you?'

He took a clean folded handkerchief out of his pocket and stepped back into her body space, lifting her chin as he gently held the cool cotton against her lip. His eyes were unfathomable coal-black pools as they held hers. 'It doesn't have to be this way between us, Gisele,' he said in a husky tone.

She took the handkerchief from him and moved away, turning her back on him. 'It's not going to work, you know,' she said. 'Nothing is going to change my mind. I will never forgive you.'

She heard the rustle of his clothes as he moved. Then she felt his hands come down on the tops of her shoulders and her whole body shivered in reaction. She closed her eyes, summoning her resolve. Where was it? What was happening to her that she wanted to turn around and melt into the warm protection of his broad chest? 'Don't…' she said, squeezing her eyes even tighter.

'Don't what?' he asked.

'You know what,' she said, suppressing a sigh of delight when his fingers began to massage the tightly knotted muscles of her neck and shoulders. If he was running true to form, any minute now he would slip the wrap from one of her shoulders and press his warm lips to her needy flesh. God help her if he did. She would have no power left in her to resist him.

'You want me, Gisele.' His still-aroused body brushed against hers from behind.

'You think.'

'I know.'

She turned and glared at him hotly. 'I want this month to be over so I can finally be free of you.'

His eyes roved her face, looking for what, she wasn't quite sure. She schooled her features into cool indifference, her version of it anyway. 'You should go to bed,' he said, brushing his thumb ever so gently against her bottom lip. 'It's a long flight tomorrow, even when travelling First Class.'

'What?' she said with a mocking look. 'No private jet any more?'

His expression remained inscrutable. 'Owning a private jet is no longer my measure of a successful person,' he said. 'I have other things I would rather spend my money on.'

'Such as?'

His hand dropped from her face as he stepped back from her. 'Good night,' he said. 'I'll see you in the morning.'

'It *is* morning,' she said, just to be pedantic and annoying, but it was a wasted effort on her part as he had already left the room.

CHAPTER FOUR

OF COURSE she didn't sleep. Not even the chemical cocktail the doctor had prescribed to help dull the nightmares about Lily had any effect on her tonight. Gisele
tossed and turned and watched as the clock went round,
her mind racing with thoughts of Emilio and the month
ahead and how on earth she was going to get through it.

In the end she gave up. She padded over to her suitcase and took out Lily's blanket and cradled it against
her chest as if her tiny baby were still alive and breathing, wrapped inside it. Tears rolled down her cheeks un-
checked. How many nights had she spent doing exactly
this? When was this searing pain ever going to ease?

She must have dozed off for she suddenly heard the
rap of Emilio's knuckles on her door. 'Time to get up,
Gisele,' he said. 'It's 7:00 a.m.'

'I'm awake,' she called out as she struggled upright
off the bed. She put Lily's blanket safely back in her
suitcase before heading for the shower.

Emilio was pouring himself a cup of coffee when Gisele
came in. She had a stoic look about her as if she were
being led to the gallows and was determined not to beg
for last-minute mercy. 'Sleep OK?' he asked.

'Out like a light.'

He doubted it. She had damson-coloured shadows under her eyes and her face was deathly pale. 'You should have something to eat,' he said, waving a hand towards the food he'd had delivered to the suite.

'I'm not hungry.'

He drew in a breath. 'You think by going on a hunger strike that it's going to help things?'

She shot him a glare. 'I'm not on a hunger strike. I'm just not hungry.'

'You're never hungry,' he snapped at her in annoyance. 'It's not normal. You need food. You'll fade away to nothing if you don't eat.'

'What would you care?' she asked. 'Your last girlfriend was much thinner than me. It *was* a swimwear model you were dating last month, wasn't it? Or have I got her mixed up with that London socialite with the big boobs?' She tapped a finger against the side of her mouth as if trying to prod her memory. 'What was her name again? Arabella? Amanda? Ariel?'

Emilio ground his teeth as he pulled out a chair for her. 'Sit.'

She gave him a castigating look. 'You know you could have saved yourself a heap of money by buying a dog to obey your commands.'

'I thought it would be much more fun training you,' he said through tight lips. 'Now, sit and eat.'

She sat with a toss of her head. 'At least I don't pee on the carpet,' she said.

'I wouldn't put it past you,' he muttered.

She picked up a rasher of bacon and dropped it on

her plate. 'So did you sleep?' she asked. 'You don't look like it. You look like hell.'

'Thank you.'

She stabbed the bacon with her fork. 'You're welcome.'

Emilio watched her as she nibbled at the bacon. Her small white teeth and those luscious lips of hers had kept him awake for what had been left of last night. He tore his gaze away and refilled his coffee cup. 'Do you want coffee or tea?' he asked.

'Tea,' she said and, rolling her eyes, added, 'Sorry for being so *un*-Italian.'

'You're not sorry at all,' he said, putting a steaming cup of tea in front of her. 'Do you want milk or sugar?'

She raised her brows at him. 'You don't remember how I take my tea?' she asked. 'Or have there been so many women since me you're getting us all a little mixed up?'

Emilio pressed his lips together. He wasn't proud of how many women there had been. It was just like her to twist the knife as much as she could. 'You take it black with one sugar,' he said.

She pressed her finger to the table and made a buzzing noise like that on a game show. 'Wrong answer.'

He frowned. 'Are you sure?'

She gave him a look. 'Yeah, I'm sure.'

'So when did you give up the sugar?' he asked.

'I did that when I was…' She stopped and dropped her gaze to her plate.

'When you were?' he prompted.

She pushed back from the table. 'I have to get my things together,' she said. 'I haven't packed.'

'You haven't unpacked,' he pointed out wryly.

'I have to do my…my hair,' she said, ruffling it with one of her hands. 'It's a mess.'

'It looked perfectly fine until you just did that,' he said.

'I have to do my make-up.'

'You're wearing make-up,' he said.

She bit her lip and then winced and put her fingers up to her mouth.

Emilio felt his gut clench. 'Does it hurt?' he asked.

Her eyes fell away from his. 'I've felt worse pain.'

A little silence passed.

'I'm sorry,' he said heavily.

'For what?' she asked, shooting him another cut glass look. 'Buying me back into your life or throwing me out of it in the first place?'

Emilio held her brittle gaze for a lengthy moment. 'I have already told you I'm not proud of how I handled things back then. This is my chance to make it up to you.' He let out a rough-edged sigh. 'It must have been terrible for you the night I asked you to leave.'

'It wasn't a highlight of my time in Italy, that's for sure,' she said, affecting a couldn't-care-less pose. 'But what doesn't kill you makes you stronger, right?'

Emilio swept his gaze over her thin frame. 'You don't look stronger, *cara*,' he said softly. 'You act it but you don't look it.'

She seemed to be actively avoiding his eyes. 'I'd really prefer it if you didn't call me that,' she said.

'I always called you that in the past.'

'This is not the past,' she said tightly. 'This is now. It's different now.'

'Not so different,' he said. 'We are together again.'

She flashed him a defiant glare. 'Only for a month.'

He picked up his coffee and took a sip before he responded. 'Maybe you'll like it so much you'll change your mind and stay.'

'And do what?' she asked. 'Hang off your arm and your every word like some besotted bimbo with no mind of her own? No, thanks. I've grown up. I want more for my life than to be a rich man's plaything.'

Emilio buttoned down his anger with an effort. 'You were going to be my wife, not my plaything,' he said.

Her eyes clashed with his. 'Why did you ask me to marry you, Emilio?' she asked. 'Why not one of the many other women you'd been involved with before me? Why was I so special?'

He put his coffee cup down with a little thwack. 'I think you already know the answer to that, Gisele.'

'It was because I was a virgin, wasn't it?' she asked. 'What a novelty in this day and age to have a woman no one else had ever had. I was a perfect candidate as your future wife. I was perfect until that scandal broke and then suddenly I wasn't worth anything to you. I was soiled. Used goods. Imperfect. And there's nothing you like less than imperfection, is there?'

Emilio pushed himself away from the counter, the set to his mouth grim. 'We need to leave in less than an hour,' he said. 'I hope I don't need to remind you that your behaviour towards me will be under intense scrutiny as soon as we leave the privacy of this hotel. I will not tolerate your insults or your childish attempts to pick a fight in front of any member of my staff, or the press, or indeed the public. If you want to have a showdown with me, then at least have the decency and poise to keep a lid on it until we are alone.'

Gisele looked at him in alarm. 'You don't expect me to act as if I'm still in love with you, do you?'

He gave her a look that would have sliced through steel. 'That's exactly what I expect,' he said. 'We're meant to be trying to resurrect our relationship.'

She felt her stomach shift uneasily. 'I can't do it,' she said. 'I can't pretend to feel something I no longer feel.'

'You will have to,' he said implacably. 'I'm not paying two million dollars for you to look daggers at me while the whole world looks on. If you can't meet the terms, then tell me now and I'll tear up the agreement. It's up to you.'

Gisele hesitated, caught between wanting to walk away and wanting to prove something to him and to herself. Could she do it? Could she act the role she had played for real with such embarrassing enthusiasm in the past? It was just a month. Four weeks of playing for the press. In private she could be herself. She could hate him a thousandfold and no one would be the wiser. 'All right,' she said, mentally crossing her fingers that she was doing the right thing. 'I'll do it.'

Thankfully, the Australian press had not been present when Gisele and Emilio left the hotel for their flight. But it was a completely different story when they landed in the Leonardo da Vinci Airport in Rome. As soon as they stepped through Customs the paparazzi swarmed like bees. Gisele felt under siege as it brought back horrible reminders of the time when the scandal had broken. The camera flashes made her flinch, and her heart was racing so much she felt as if she was going to faint.

She had pretended to sleep on the plane rather than try and make polite conversation with Emilio, but it was all catching up with her now. She felt tired and sick and way too much out of her depth to cope with the barrage of comments firing like machine gun bullets at her. She had always found the intrusion of the press rather daunting from the moment she became involved with Emilio. She had felt as if she was under scrutiny all the time. The speculation on what she wore, how she looked or whether she was smiling or frowning was something she had never got used to. Rumours about their relationship would appear from time to time, which Emilio had laughed off, but Gisele—although she had pretended otherwise—had been distressed by the lack of privacy.

Emilio spoke in Italian, asking the press to keep back to give Gisele some room. His arm came around her protectively, and if it hadn't been for their terse exchange before they left the hotel, Gisele would have been tempted to believe he truly cared about her welfare rather than his reputation.

'Signor Andreoni—' a journalist pushed through the cluster of cameras with a microphone '—does this mean you and Signorina Carter will be getting married as soon as possible?'

'We are enjoying some time together before we make any firm plans,' Emilio answered.

Gisele had learnt a bit of Italian while she had lived with Emilio but it wasn't enough to follow every rapidly spoken word, although she did hear the word *matri-*

monio—marriage. What exactly was he telling the press?

'Signorina Carter?' The same journalist turned the microphone in Gisele's direction but this time spoke in English. 'Is it good to be back with Signor Andreoni?'

Gisele stumbled over her reply. 'Um… I'm very happy…'

'It has been two years since your very public break-up,' the journalist continued. 'You must be feeling very relieved the truth has finally come out about who exactly it was in that sex tape.'

Gisele felt uncomfortable talking about her sister's private life. Sienna had seemed reluctant to go into any details other than to say the press had blown it up to be much more than it actually was. Gisele suspected that ignominious incident had been devastating for her twin, although Sienna pretended otherwise. 'I'm happy that I've found my sister,' she said. 'That's been the most important outcome of such a difficult time.'

'Is your twin sister planning on spending some time with you now that you are going to be living in Italy?' another journalist asked.

'I'm not planning on stay—'

Emilio cut Gisele off. 'We are both looking forward to spending time with Sienna Baker. Now, if you will excuse us, we have to get moving.'

'Signorina Carter, one more question…' Yet another journalist rushed after them.

'Basta,' Emilio said and then repeated it in English. 'That's enough.'

He spirited her away to the waiting car, physically blocking the swarm of press as she got in. 'Remember what I said earlier about what you do and say to me in public,' he said.

Gisele caught the driver's watchful eye in the rear-view mirror. A glass partition separated her and Emilio from the front of the car but it was hardly what one would call being in private. She forced herself to sit with a relaxed pose beside Emilio even though she wished she had the courage to thrust open the door and throw herself out of his life, both literally and figuratively.

She drew in a sharp little breath as she looked out at the scenery passing by. The Colosseum suddenly appeared and a tight ache settled in her chest. She could still remember the excitement of her first trip to Italy after she had met Emilio while she was doing a needle-work course at the London School of Embroidery. They had met at an art exhibition she had been invited to by one of the girls she had met doing her course, whose boyfriend couldn't make it at the last minute. Gisele had been in two minds whether or not to attend but in the end had decided to go so that her new friend wouldn't have to go alone. Within minutes of walking into the small privately owned gallery she had met Emilio's gaze from across the room. She could still recall the way her heart had fluttered in her chest as he moved through the knot of people to get to her. He had been head and shoulders above all the other men, not just in stature, but also in looks and in his proud, almost aristocratic bearing. She had thought he must be Italian royalty at the very least, and why he should single her out was beyond her comprehension. But single her out he had, and within a week she had been swept off her feet and totally, blissfully in love.

'I have a new housekeeper,' Emilio said into the silence that had fallen. 'Her name is Marietta.'

'What happened to Concetta?' Gisele asked with a frown.

His mouth tightened briefly. 'I fired her the day after you left.'

'Why?' she asked. 'I thought you said she was the best housekeeper you'd ever had.'

'She was.'

'So why'd you fire her?'

'She overstepped the mark in telling me I was a fool for throwing you out,' he said. 'I fired her on the spot.'

'Way to go, Concetta,' Gisele said. She pushed her tongue against the inside of her bottom lip as she studied his brooding expression. 'You didn't think to ask her to come back to you along with me?'

His brows moved together over his eyes as he looked at her. 'She wouldn't come back,' he said.

Gisele gave him a saccharine-sweet smile. 'Maybe you should've offered her two million dollars.'

He didn't answer but she saw his jaw flex just before he turned and looked out of the window.

The driver pulled up in front of Emilio's villa in the exclusive area near the Villa Borghese parklands. Gisele felt another pang as Emilio helped her from the car. She had been totally blown away by the magnificent building two years ago and she felt exactly the same way now. Built on four levels with gorgeous formal gardens and a huge fountain set in the middle of the circular driveway, it looked every inch the private residence of a person who had very much made their way in the world.

Emilio gave the driver instructions about their luggage before leading Gisele to the front door, which magically opened, revealing a neatly dressed Italian woman in her fifties with a welcoming but deferential smile on her face. '*Bentornati,* Signorina Carter,' she said. 'Welcome back. Congratulations on renewing your engagement.'

'*Grazie,*' Gisele said, taking the housekeeper's hand and returning her smile with an effort. *Engagement? What engagement?* Anger bubbled up inside her. What on earth did Emilio think he was doing? She could hardly have it out with him in front of the housekeeper. She stood with a frozen smile on her face, furious with him for putting her in such an invidious position.

Emilio spoke to Marietta in Italian before turning to Gisele. 'Marietta will unpack your things while you have a rest,' he said.

Gisele faltered as she thought of Lily's blanket inside her case. 'Um… Do you mind if I do it myself? I haven't brought much with me anyway. I feel…um… embarrassed. I need some new clothes. There hasn't been much money for extras just lately…'

He studied her flushed features for a pulsing moment, his eyes dark and unreadable. 'You have no need to be embarrassed,' he said. 'I will see to it that you have all the clothes you need.'

'I'd still like to unpack my own things,' she said. 'I've got out of the habit of having people waiting on me.'

He held her look for another beat or two. 'As you wish.'

Gisele let out a breath of relief as he turned and issued Marietta another set of instructions. She didn't want anyone handling Lily's blanket. No one had touched it but her. She didn't want to lose that last trace of her baby's scent…

Emilio turned back and took Gisele's hand and toyed with the knuckle of her ring finger as he held her gaze. 'We have a little job to do, *sì*?' he said. 'I have your engagement ring in the safe in my study.'

'So you managed to fish it out of the fountain, then?' she asked with an arch look.

'It took three plumbers, but yes,' he said. 'I finally managed to locate it.'

Gisele waited until they were alone in the study where his safe was before she let fly. 'How *could* you lead your housekeeper to believe that we're engaged? I haven't agreed to that! I've only agreed to come here for a month but not as your fiancée.'

Emilio's expression remained calm, as if he were dealing with a small, wilful child. 'Relax, *cara*,' he said. 'There is no need for such hysterics.'

'I am *not* hysterical!' Gisele shrieked with a stamp of her foot for good measure.

His brows snapped together. 'Keep your voice down.'

She clenched her hands into fists and spoke through tight lips. 'You've done this deliberately, haven't you? You're making it impossible for me to deny we have a formal relationship by making me wear your stupid ring.'

'*Cara*, you're tired and overwrought,' he said. 'You're not making sense. Of course you will have to wear my ring while you are here. People will not accept our reconciliation as the real thing if we don't appear to pick up where we left off.'

She glowered at him. 'You think by putting that ring on my finger it gives you automatic licence to sleep with me, don't you?'

'You will sleep with me, ring or no ring,' he said. 'We will be sharing my room. I will not have it any other way. I don't want the servants to suspect anything is amiss.'

Gisele's heart tripped in her chest like a pony's hoof in a pothole. 'I'd rather sleep on the floor than share a bed with you.'

'It seems to me you don't sleep anywhere,' he returned wryly. 'Your little closed-eye routine didn't fool me on the flight, *cara*. That's obviously why you're being so obstreperous now. You're acting like a little child who has been kept up way past her bedtime.'

She swung away from him in fury, flustered because he saw too damn much. She was worried because she didn't trust herself not to turn to him during the night. If her nightmares about Lily hadn't been enough to deal with, so many times over the past two years she had found herself reaching for him during that half-awake, half-asleep phase of fitful rest. Her need for him had not automatically switched off just because he had thrown her out of his life. If anything, it had smouldered under the surface, building in intensity as each lonely month had passed.

Gisele heard the sound of the safe being opened and drew in a breath for composure. This would be another emotional hurdle for her to negotiate. How different would this be from when he had slid that ring onto her finger after he had asked her to marry him? She didn't want to think about how eagerly and excitedly she had accepted his proposal. She had gushed in enthusiasm and he had looked down at her with the sort of indulgent amusement that made her cringe now. How gauche she had been, how foolishly romantic to think he had adored her even a fraction as much as she had adored him. He hadn't loved her at all. She had simply ticked all the boxes for him under the compartment in his life marked: Find Suitable Wife.

'Give me your hand,' Emilio commanded.

Gisele turned around like a statue on a plinth, her body tense from head to foot. 'I don't suppose you're going to do a rerun of your proposal?' she said.

His eyes glinted as he took her hand in his. 'I had thought of it but decided against it.'

'Why?' she asked. 'Because you were worried I'd say no?'

He slid the ring onto her finger, holding it there with the warmth of his finger and thumb, his eyes still meshed with hers. 'Ah, but *would* you say no?' he asked.

'Why don't you give it a shot and see?' she challenged him.

He gave a little chuckle that was spine-tinglingly deep. 'I'm sure if the price was right you would agree to marry me,' he said, bringing her hand up to his mouth and pressing his lips against her bent fingers.

Gisele felt a butterfly wing–like flutter pass over the floor of her belly. She disguised a swallow as she felt his lips move to the sensitive skin of the underside of her wrist. She wanted to close her eyes and lose herself in his magical touch. The sensation of his warm velvet lips made her skin shiver in reaction. 'Stop it,' she said, not really meaning it and pretty sure he knew it.

He slid his tongue over her leaping pulse, a sexy lick that sent a dart of pleasure straight to her core. She suppressed a tiny whimper, determined not to show him how much he affected her by his proximity, by his touch, by his astonishing ability to dismantle her defences. Her legs felt like dampened paper, barely strong enough to hold her upright. Her spine was loosening, vertebra by vertebra, until she felt sure she would melt into a pool at his feet. Where was her resolve? Where was her anger when she needed it? They were like cowardly soldiers retreating from the frontline of battle.

'You taste like summer,' Emilio said against her wrist. 'Like frangipani and honeysuckle.'

Gisele shivered as his teeth gave her a playful but gentle bite. Her breasts peaked with longing, her insides contracting with need. How was she going to resist him if he kept this up? It was torture to be so near him and not respond the way she wanted to. 'I need a shower...' she said.

'Have one with me.'

The images those words conjured up! She had to fight with everything within her to keep them from flooding her mind. But it was impossible to eradicate every single one. She felt the heat build inside her at the memory of his hard body driving into her as the water cascaded over them: the memory of his hot, clever mouth feasting on her intimately and the memory of her doing exactly the same to him. Just thinking about the earthy rawness of it made her cheeks grow warm. 'I don't think so,' she said, trying to pull away.

His eyes came back to hers as he held her firm. 'It

won't be long before you change your mind, *cara*. We both know that, don't we?'

She glared at him, spitting out the words one by one. 'Let. Me. Go.'

He pulled her up against him, pressing a brief hard kiss to her mouth before he released her. 'Go and have your rest,' he said. 'I'll see you at dinner.'

Gisele felt unsettled and disoriented when he stepped away from her. It was a feeling almost like being cast adrift. She felt strangely empty without his hands holding her against him. That too-brief kiss had made her feel hungry for more. She swept the tip of her tongue over the tingling surface of her lips, the tantalising taste of him making her insides clench with longing. She didn't realise she was still standing there in a zombie-like daze until she heard the soft click of the study door, signalling Emilio had left.

Walking back into Emilio's bedroom suite was something Gisele had been silently dreading for all the memories being there would stir up, but when she pushed open the door she was surprised to see everything had changed. The decor was completely different, even the bed ensemble and the light fittings and soft furnishings. She wondered if he had done it deliberately, somehow purging his room of her presence after he had sent her from his life.

The master suite now had a Venetian theme to it with the boldest of gold and black in the fabric of the curtains and bed linen. Crystal lamps encrusted with onyx and gold were stationed either side of the massive bed, and the priceless thick carpet on the floor continued the theme.

The en suite bathroom was fitted out in highly polished black marble with gold tap wear and golden-framed mirrors. There was a large shower with two showerheads and a deep marble-surrounded bath and a heated towel rack with several snowy-white towels with a black-and-gold trim neatly folded there.

It was decadent and rich and luxurious, the perfect setting for seduction, Gisele thought as she came back to the windows that led out onto a balcony that overlooked the gardens.

She opened the French windows and went out to breathe in the warm spring air, the clovelike scent of roses drifting towards her from below. The rear gardens were much the same as before, lots of clipped hedges and herbaceous borders and roses everywhere. A lavender pathway led to another fountain, larger than the one at the front. The sound of the water splashing had always had a soporific effect on her. She had spent many nights lying in Emilio's arms listening to that wonderfully relaxing sound as she drifted off to sleep, dreaming of their future together...

She stepped out of her reverie by leaving the balcony and closing the doors, turning the key as a reminder to herself that the past was no longer accessible.

She found another room farther down the hall. It was decorated in tones of milky coffee and white, with large windows overlooking the gardens.

Once she unpacked her things from her suitcase and stored them in the wardrobe, she found a drawer to put Lily's blanket and photos in and gently closed it.

The aching tiredness she felt was suddenly so over-whelming she was barely aware of kicking off her shoes before she curled up like a comma on the feather-soft bed and closed her eyes…

Emilio searched through several bedrooms before he found Gisele lying sound asleep on the bed in the room furthest from his. Her silver-blonde hair was spread out over the pillow, her slim body barely making an indentation on the mattress. She looked like an angel lying there, a sleeping angel with features so perfect and yet so pale she didn't seem quite real. How was he to get through the wall of her anger? He had to dismantle it brick by brick, getting her to slowly warm to him again.

Looking back now, he could see how truly devastated she had been when he had cast her from his life. At the time he had read her body language as a greedy little gold-digger whose plans to wed a rich man had been thwarted at the last minute, but now he could see her shattered expression for what it was: a young woman who had loved and loved deeply, who by a quirk of fate had suddenly found her life in ruins through no fault of her own.

Where had she gone?

Who had she turned to?

How must she have felt to have her life ripped out from under her without warning? He didn't like thinking about it. She would have been feeling so shocked and frightened, so upset that she hadn't been able to get him to see reason. Even worse, anything could have happened to her that night. In her state of high emotional distress she could have come to some sort of harm and he had done nothing to protect her. He had cast her out of his life as if she had been nothing more than some trash he no longer had any use for.

He had got it so horribly wrong.

Emilio watched the soft flutter of her lips as she gave an inaudible murmur and the way one of her hands seemed to be searching for something on the bed next to her. Her face suddenly contorted as if she was having a terrible nightmare. She started to thrash about, her cries soft but heart-wrenching. 'No…oh, no, please *no*…'

'Gisele, shh, it's all right,' Emilio said softly as he perched beside her and captured her flailing hands.

Her eyes sprang open and she jerked upright. She seemed momentarily disoriented but then her expression turned hostile. 'What are you doing here?' she asked, pulling her hands away from his.

'I hate to point out the obvious, but this is my villa and you are in one of my bedrooms,' Emilio said.

She brushed her hair out of her eyes with an angry movement of her hand as she gave him a resentful scowl. 'You shouldn't sneak up on people like that,' she said.

'I didn't sneak up on you,' he said. 'It looked like you were having a bad dream. You were crying out in your sleep so I came over to comfort you.'

She bit down on her lower lip, a soft flush rising in her cheeks as she averted her gaze from his.

Emilio turned her chin so she had to meet his eyes. 'Do you often have bad dreams, *cara*?' he asked.

A shadow passed over her blue eyes. 'Not often… sometimes…'

He caressed her cheek with the pad of his thumb.

'I wish I could wipe out the last two years,' he said. 'I wish I could just reset the clock. I wish I could take back every horrible word I threw at you.'

She didn't answer. She just kept looking at him with that grey-blue accusing gaze of hers.

'What did you do the night I sent you away?' Emilio asked.

'I found a hotel,' she said. 'The press gave me a hard time but eventually I managed to shake them off. I caught a flight back to Sydney the next day.'

'You never tried to contact me,' he said, still stroking her creamy cheek. 'Not even once.'

She gave him a brittle look. 'You forbade me to, remember?'

He studied her for a long moment before dropping his hand from her chin. 'Dinner is in half an hour,' he said as he rose from the bed. 'I'll see you downstairs.'

CHAPTER FIVE

AFTER Gisele had a shower she dressed in a slim-fitting sheathlike taupe-coloured dress and a pair of heels. She dried her hair and scooped it up into a knot at the back of her head and put on a bare minimum of make-up. She looked down at the engagement ring on her finger. It was too loose for her now. The huge diamond kept slipping round the wrong way out of sight. Was that some sort of omen? she wondered.

Emilio was in the *salone* when she came downstairs. He was sipping at an aperitif, looking out of the window to the gardens outside. He turned and looked at her, his gaze moving over her body like a warm caress. 'You look beautiful,' he said.

'Thank you.' Gisele fought for cool poise but a blush crept over her cheeks in spite of her best efforts.

'What would you like to drink?' he asked.

'Um…white wine if you have it.'

He poured her a glass of wine and brought it over to her. She saw his nostrils flare as if he was taking in the fragrance of her perfume. She saw too the way his eyes darkened as they caught and held hers. 'Do you feel a little more refreshed after your rest?' he asked.

'Yes,' she said, taking a generous sip to settle her nerves.

'Why didn't you put your things in my bedroom as I asked you to?' he said.

She gripped her wineglass a little tighter. 'You can't force me to occupy your bed. I need more time. It's a big step for me.'

'Didn't you like the new decor?' he asked.

'It looks like no expense has been spared to rid your bedroom of every trace of my previous occupation of it,' Gisele said with a touch of asperity.

His expression was unreadable as he raised his glass to his lips. 'I thought it was time for a change.'

'Out with the old, in with the new?' she said with a cynical look. 'Did all your subsequent girlfriends like it?'

A brooding frown appeared between his eyebrows. 'If you don't like it then we can occupy another room,' he said. 'But you *will* share a bed with me, Gisele. I will not have any rumours circulating that this is not a proper relationship.'

'How soon did you replace me?' she asked.

A muscle worked in his jaw. 'Gisele, this is not going to help matters.'

'How many?' she asked, feeling a lump rise in her throat.

'I could ask you the same thing.'

'Go on,' she said. 'Ask me.'

The muscle in his jaw worked even harder. 'All right,' he said on an expelled breath. 'How many lovers have you had since me?'

Gisele wished now she hadn't provoked him. Could

she lie just to hurt him? Could she play payback with a host of imaginary lovers, not one of whom would have come close to being as perfect for her physically as him? What was the point? She suspected he would see through it anyway. Hadn't the way she'd responded to him so far given him enough proof that she hadn't moved on?

'There's been no one,' she said after a tight pause.

'Gisele…'

'Don't get me wrong.' She cut him off quickly. 'I've had plenty of opportunities. I just didn't want to rush into anything. You don't have to automatically assume I was waiting for you to take me back because I wasn't.'

He took his drink and moved over to the windows again, his back turned towards her. It was a moment or two before he spoke and, when he did, his voice was rough around the edges, as if it had been dragged up from a place deep inside him. 'Would you believe me if I told you I was thinking of making contact with you even before the press release came out about Sienna being the one in the tape?'

Gisele felt her heart give a little hit-and-miss beat. 'Why?'

He turned from the window and faced her with an inscrutable look. 'I'm not sure,' he said. 'I guess I wanted to see if you had fared any better than me.'

'What do you mean?'

'Anger and bitterness are pretty corrosive things to be carrying around,' he said. 'I think I got tired of being angry. For two years I was totally consumed with it. I could think of nothing else. I finally got to the point where I wanted to move on. I thought if I contacted you, perhaps met with you face to face to ask you why you'd betrayed me, it might've helped.'

'But I hadn't betrayed you.'

He let out a heavy sigh. 'No,' he said. 'You hadn't. And that's what I have to live with. I made a mistake. It's new territory for me. I'm not usually wrong about anything.'

Gisele looked at the wine in her glass and thought about what he had said about carrying around anger. Her anger had burned like acid inside her. It was still burning, eating away at her, keeping her awake at night. But she wasn't quite ready to relinquish it.

Marietta appeared at that point with the announcement that dinner was ready.

Gisele followed Emilio to the dining room where the long highly polished table had been beautifully set up for a romantic dinner for two. Flowers from the garden made a fragrant centrepiece along with the flickering candles in the candelabra that added to the tone of intimacy. So many times in the past she had sat here at this table and looked lovingly across the table at him. She had pictured their children one day joining them there, their little faces shining with good health and happiness and vigour. How far from her dreams and romantically infused imaginings had she travelled? There would be no happy family now. Not for her at least.

Emilio seated her before he took his own place. 'I've been thinking about your business,' he said. 'Do you outsource any of the needlework?'

'No,' she said. 'I do it all myself. I like working to commission. I think it gives the customer that sense of a personal touch.'

He reached across to pour her some wine. 'But you surely can't expect to keep up with demand if things were to take a sudden upswing?'

'I've managed to keep ahead so far.'

'Yes, but that will change as soon as things take off over here,' he said. 'How will you keep up then?'

She bit her lip. 'I've brought some work with me...'

'Gisele.' He sounded like a world-weary parent speaking to a naive child. 'You can't expect to run things as you have done in the past. You'll have to consider outsourcing. You have no choice. You can hand-pick your needlewomen. You'll still have total control over the standard of your product.'

She flashed him a defensive glare. 'I know what I'm doing. I'm good at what I do. I love my work.'

'The creative side of it is not the problem, *cara*,' he said. 'I've seen your needlework. It's exquisite. You are extremely talented. I'm not saying you aren't. I'm just saying you can't possibly do it all. You need to think about how to meet demands for more of your work, otherwise people will go elsewhere.'

Gisele pressed her lips together before answering. 'OK, I'll think about it.'

He gave a sigh and reached for her hand across the table. 'Look at me, *cara*,' he commanded gently.

She met his gaze with resentment burning in hers. 'I won't allow you to take over my life. I've been doing perfectly fine without you. My shop is the busiest one on that stretch of the street.'

'I know that,' he said. 'You've done amazingly well. I'm just trying to help you do better, to maximise your profits. At least if things don't work out between us you will have a stronger base to go home to.'

Marietta came in with their meal and Emilio deftly steered the conversation into less contentious areas. Gisele made an effort to do the delicious food justice but being in Emilio's presence made her feel nervous and excited at the same time. He could be such charming company when he put his mind to it. She felt the intoxicating lure of it each time he looked at her with that sexy slant of a smile. His eyes took on a dark mesmerising heat as they held hers, the sensual promise in them making every hair on her body stand up and take notice.

After Marietta had served coffee in the *salone* she announced she was leaving for home.

'She doesn't live here like Concetta did?' Gisele asked once the housekeeper had left.

'No,' Emilio said. 'She has a husband and a couple of daughters who still live at home. She likes to spend the nights with them.'

'So if she's not here at night then there should be no problem with me having my own room,' Gisele said.

His expression tightened. 'She is back first thing in the morning,' he said. 'What are you going to do? Run along the hall and jump in beside me just for show?'

She put her coffee cup down and rose to her feet agitatedly. The thought of jumping into bed with him for real was far too tempting. It was all she could think about. Her body burned with hot flames of need and there was nothing she could do to dampen them down. 'Lots of couples don't sleep together,' she said. 'My parents didn't share a bed for most of their marriage.'

He came over to where she was standing. 'That is not how this relationship is going to be run,' he said. He took her hands in his and held them gently but firmly. 'Why are you fighting what is inevitable? I know you were hurt by our break-up. I understand that you're still angry. We have this chance to reconnect but you seem intent on sabotaging every attempt on my part to put things right.'

'Some things can never be put right,' she said, looking down at their joined hands rather than meeting his gaze. Her belly quivered as his thumbs began stroking her fingers, his darker-toned skin against hers a spine-tingling reminder of how very masculine he was and how she couldn't help but respond to his primal call to all that was feminine in her. She could feel the flicker of desire between her thighs, a tiny rhythmic pulse that was like a faraway drumbeat deep inside her, each throbbing second bringing it closer and closer…

Emilio tipped up her chin, his eyes so dark she couldn't make out his pupils. 'Are you fighting me or yourself, *cara*?' he asked.

She sent the point of her tongue out over her lips, testing his hold but it remained firm. 'I hate you,' she said, but somehow the words didn't sound as feisty and determined as they had even a day ago.

'That doesn't mean that the sex between us won't still be good,' he said as his mouth blazed a hot trail over the sensitive skin near her left ear.

Gisele felt her senses go into a tailspin as his teeth gently tugged on her earlobe. It sent a delicious shiver down her spine as he moved back towards her mouth, slowly, tantalisingly, awakening each and every nerve beneath her skin, making her lips tingle in anticipation for the hot, urgent pressure of his. She gave a soft little whimper and turned her head just a fraction, just enough to make that final devastating contact.

His mouth sealed hers but it was nothing like the bruising kiss of the other day. This was a kiss that was sensually soft, exploratory and yet unmistakably commanding and arrantly sexual in its intent. She felt the stroke of his tongue at the seam of her lips and she opened to him, their breaths mingling, their tongues mating in an erotic ritual that sent lightning bolts of need straight to the heart of her femininity. One of his hands slipped to the nape of her neck, the warm cup of his palm causing the entire length of her spine to shudder in delicious response. His mouth changed position, his lips still moving gently against hers, but she still sensed an undercurrent of urgency, of his control still tightly leashed but straining for freedom.

His other hand pressed her in the small of her back, bringing her closer to the pulsing heat of his erection. She felt its thickness, the potent power of it stirring her body into a maelstrom of feeling. Her skin tightened, her heart fluttered, her legs trembled and still the kiss went on and on.

It was so wonderful to *feel* again. To feel alive and vibrant with sexual energy, to feel the way her body inflamed his by its closeness. His hand at her back pressed harder, a low groan emitting from his throat as she rubbed against him, her feminine mound aching to feel his possession. It was a deep ache inside her, a pulsing, throbbing ache that she could feel vibrating in his body as he ground himself against her, hungry for relief.

'I want you,' he growled like a wolf against her mouth, the primal deepness of his voice and the scrape of his teeth as he tugged at her lower lip making Gisele melt like honey under intense heat.

She didn't need to say she wanted him too. Her body was doing all it could to relay the message of how much she needed him to relieve her of this voracious need that was clawing at her insides. She pushed herself closer, her breasts jammed up against the hard wall of his chest, her mouth feeding greedily off his.

Emilio pulled down the zip of her dress, his hands moving over the naked skin of her back in tantalising strokes that made her legs feel as if they were going to go out from beneath her. He deftly unhooked her bra and it slid to the floor along with her dress, leaving her in nothing but her knickers and her heels. He brought his mouth to her achingly tight breast, sucking on her erect nipple before doing the same to the other. Gisele whimpered as her senses screamed in rapture. It was so good to feel him on her naked flesh, to feel the sexy rasp of his masculine jaw with its pepper of stubble on her soft skin.

She took her hands from around his neck and worked her way down his shirt, button by button, tasting the sexy saltiness of his skin with her tongue, teasing each of his flat male nipples with her teeth. He shrugged himself out of his shirt as she moved her hands down to the waistband of his trousers. She ran her hand over the proud jut of his body, her insides clenching with feverish anticipation as he moved against her hand with a guttural groan.

'I knew you would come back to me,' Emilio said in a gravel-rough tone as his lips hovered above her mouth. 'I knew you wouldn't be able to resist.'

The ice-cold water of common sense doused the flames of Gisele's desire at the hint of arrogant assurance in his tone. Did he really think she was *that* predictable? That he only had to beckon to her and she would come running back as if nothing had happened? 'Wait,' she said, dropping her hands from his body.

He frowned at her. 'Is everything all right?'

Gisele took a deep steadying breath and covered her naked breasts with her crossed arms. 'I can't do this,' she said. 'Not like this…not here…'

'Then we'll take it upstairs,' Emilio said.

She sent him a speaking glance. 'No.'

'No?'

'I'm sorry,' she said, bending down to retrieve her dress and her bra, her cheeks so hot they felt as if they had been scorched. She got dressed with as much dignity as she could, putting some order to her hair as she faced him once more. 'I'm sorry, Emilio. I know I should have called a halt earlier. I don't know what I was thinking. Maybe I wasn't thinking. I don't seem to do a lot of that when I'm around you.' She made a self-deprecating movement of her lips. 'I guess that's one thing that hasn't changed in two years.'

He gave her a wry smile as he brushed her cheek with the tip of his index finger. 'I like it when you're not thinking,' he said. 'I like it best when you're just feeling.'

Gisele chewed at her lip. 'It's been a long time for me,' she said softly.

He cupped her cheek with the warmth of his hand, his eyes dark and surprisingly tender as they meshed with hers. 'I know,' he said. 'That's why I want our first time back together to be special. I don't want to rush things just for the sake of it. I want to savour every moment with you.'

'You sound like you missed me,' she said a little wistfully.

His thumb brushed over her bottom lip like a teasing feather. 'Those first few days after you left I was unbearable to be around,' he said. 'The contract I was working on securing fell through. The man I was negotiating with was a very conservative family man. He gave the contract to the other architect who, unfortunately, was my biggest rival. I was so blind with rage I felt sure you must have had something to do with it. I thought you had been planted as a spy.' His mouth twisted. 'I became totally obsessed after that. I had to work hard to make up for the loss of that commission. The first real block of time I've had off since then was when I flew to Sydney to see you.'

Gisele thought of him working himself to the ground in an attempt to put her out of his mind. He had always been an intensely driven man. She had recognised that when she'd first met him. It had inspired her to think of how hard he had worked for his success. He had told her once it had been his dream since childhood to become an architect and he had determined nothing would get in his way. And it hadn't. He had become one of the world's leading and most innovative designers with a string of accolades to his name.

To suddenly find out he had been wrong about the accusations he had hurled at her must have come as a horrid shock to a man with his level of pride. The fact that he had put everything on hold to fly out to see her to make amends was certainly admirable, but she still suspected it was his pride and reputation that was at stake, not his heart.

His heart was for no one. Whatever had happened in his childhood had left scars that cut deep. That was another thing Gisele had suspected right from the start, but she had been determined to be the one to heal him. How deluded had she been to think that the strength of her love could unlock his fiercely guarded heart? He had trust issues that no amount of love would ever heal. She had been a casualty of that lack of trust, and she very much doubted that she was the first or even going to be the last.

'Have you spoken to Sienna about us?' he asked.

'I didn't go into a lot of detail,' Gisele said. 'I didn't want her to feel responsible for what happened between us. You have to remember that although we're identical twins we're virtual strangers. It will take some time to get to know each other properly.'

'Do you like her?' Emilio asked. 'Is she someone you could warm to?'

Gisele thought of her vibrant, vivacious twin, with her generous and impulsive nature. From what she had picked up so far, Sienna had got herself into plenty of scrapes because of her somewhat reckless take on life, but it was impossible not to like her. 'I think she's

lovely,' she said. 'She's smart and sassy and sophisti-
cated. But I think the press misrepresent her. They paint
her as a hedonist, a wild child without morals. I don't
think she's anything like that. I think she's very sensitive but hides it behind the party girl façade.'

'I have a client to see in London towards the end of
the month,' Emilio said. 'I'd like it if you came with me.
You can introduce me to Sienna and perhaps spend some
time with her while I'm at work.'

'I'd like to see her,' Gisele said. 'But I don't want to
lie to her about our relationship. Putting on an act for
the press is one thing, lying to my sister is another.'

'Perhaps by then it won't be an act, *cara*,' he said,
brushing her lip again with his thumb.

Gisele felt the sensitive surface of her lips tingle from
the gentle caress. It was true what he had said: she was
fighting herself rather than him. Her unruly desires
were annihilating her resolve like a hurricane against a
house of cards. She had no hope of withstanding him,
not while her feelings for him were still so ambiguous.
She stepped back from him, giving him a brief on-off
smile. 'I think I'll go to bed,' she said. 'Good night.'

Emilio didn't answer but Gisele felt his scorching
gaze follow her as she left the room.

CHAPTER SIX

GISELE was pulling back the covers of her bed when she heard the bedroom door open and Emilio came in dressed in a bathrobe, his hair still damp from a recent shower. 'What do you think you're doing?' she gasped in shock.

'Coming to bed,' he said, slipping off the robe.

Gisele's eyes drank in the sight of him: that hard muscular chest, that gorgeous flat washboard abdomen and the arrantly masculine heart of him that was already partially aroused. Her heart gave a jerky kick inside her chest and her throat almost closed over. 'But I told you I—'

'And I told you how things were going to be,' he said before she could complete her sentence. 'We will share a bed for the month even if we don't make love. I will not force myself on you. You should know me better than that.'

She swallowed deeply, wondering if it was possible to share a villa of this size with Emilio without wanting to make love, let alone a bed. It was a big bed certainly, but not big enough for her to avoid those long, strong hair-roughened legs coming into contact with hers. 'That's not the point,' she said, running the tip of her tongue out over lips so dry they felt like ancient parchment.

'What *is* the point, Gisele?' he asked with a glittering look. 'You don't seem to know what you want. One minute you look at me as if you want to throw yourself back in my arms and never leave, and the next you look like you want to claw my eyes out. At some point you're going to have to make up your mind.'

Gisele had thought she had made up her mind but her body had chosen an entirely different path. It was calling out to him now in a secret sensual language he couldn't fail to misinterpret. But in her haste to disguise how much she wanted him she swung away from the bed and in doing so accidentally knocked the glass of water and her pills off the bedside table. The glass landed with a thump on the carpet and the little bottle of pills rolled across the floor and came to a stop right in front of Emilio's left foot.

She watched, dry mouthed, as he bent to pick them up. 'What are these for?' he asked, frowning as he read the label.

'Give them to me,' she said, trying to make a grab for them but he held the bottle just out of her reach.

He frowned as he read the label. 'Sleeping tablets?' he asked, looking at her again.

'So?' she said, throwing him a defensive look. 'Lots of people take them.'

'How long have you been taking them?' he asked.

Gisele folded her arms mutinously, her mouth in a flat line.

'Gisele?' He tipped up her chin, forcing her eyes to

meet his. 'How long have you been taking sleeping medication?'

She let out a shaky breath. 'A while…a few weeks…a couple of months maybe…'

'Sleeping tablets are meant to be a temporary thing,' Emilio said reprovingly. 'You shouldn't be on them any longer than a few weeks. They're highly addictive.'

Gisele rolled her eyes. 'You sound just like my doctor.'

He caught her just before she made to turn away from him. His eyes were dark and a concerned frown sliced deep into his forehead. '*Cara*, did *I* do this to you?' he asked hollowly.

Gisele thought of the weeks after his rejection when she had done nothing but sleep most days as well as the nights. She had slid into an abyss of depression that had made every little task an impossible feat. Having a shower hurt her skin. Brushing her hair felt like torture. Getting dressed in street clothes made her muscles ache. Walking to the front door had seemed like a marathon. Getting through each day felt like a lifetime. The warm, secure nest of her bed had been a reprieve from a life she didn't think she could live without him in it.

And then she had discovered she was pregnant. The news had pulled her out of her depression. She had started to look forward to life again with hope and a tentative happiness that had all too soon been torn away from her.

Was Emilio to blame that Lily had died?

For a while she had felt as if he was, but over time she had come to realise no one was to blame. It was just

one of those things, or so the doctors had said—a genetic abnormality, a mistake of nature.

'No…' Gisele said in a voice so soft it was more of a
whisper. 'No, it's not because of you.' It was the sound
of Lily crying that haunted her sleepless nights. The
only way to escape the torture of hearing that tiny mewling cry was to numb herself to sleep. Not that it always
worked.

Emilio looked deeply into her eyes as if he wanted to
see into the very heart of her. His eyes were pitch-black,
still etched with concern as he cupped her face. 'Is it
because of the business? Your father's death? Finding
out about Sienna?'

Gisele put her hand on his to peel it off her face and
stepped backwards, wrapping her arms about her body.
Should she tell him about Lily? She could feel guilt nip-
ping at the heels of her conscience. Didn't he have the
right to know he had been a father, even for such a short
time? She would have to tell him one day. What if he
somehow found out by some other means? The thought
was terrifying. Wouldn't it be better to hear it from her
rather than someone else? But how could she drop that
sort of bombshell into the conversation? Her chance to
tell him had been right at the start. She couldn't talk
about it now. Not like this, with no preparation. 'I…I've
just been under a lot of stress,' she said. 'It's no one thing
but everything, I guess.'

'You should wean yourself off them,' he said, still
frowning. 'I don't like the thought of you drugging
yourself to sleep. You never used to have any problem
sleeping.'

She gave him a wry look before she could stop herself. 'As I recall, we didn't always do a lot of sleeping.'

The words seemed to hang in the air for a moment, the erotic images they conjured up gathering around like ghosts from the past.

Gisele saw the flare of heat in Emilio's eyes as he took in her scantily clad body. She had slipped off her wrap just before he had come in and her creamy satin nightgown left very little to the imagination. She felt the tight buds of her nipples pressing against the soft fabric and knew he could see them too. Her belly gave an excited flutter as his eyes skimmed her lower body, the heat in her core liquefying as if he had touched her there. His body responded to her as if she had stroked her fingers along his length. She saw him swell and rise, the sheer power and potency of him taking her breath away.

'No, we didn't, did we?' Emilio asked with a smouldering look as his eyes slowly came back to mesh with hers.

Gisele drew in a quick breath, her chest feeling prickly and tight. The heat from his body radiated out and touched her like a caress. Her skin felt tingly and supersensitive, as if all the nerves had repositioned themselves on the outside of her body. 'Don't do this, Emilio,' she said in a hoarse whisper.

'Don't do what, *cara*?' he asked as he shrank the gap between their bodies by taking half a step. 'This?' He touched his lips to the skin of her neck just below her ear, not a kiss, not a bite, but something sinfully and sexily in between.

She shivered as his tongue grazed her skin as he

moved down to the fragile scaffold of her collarbone. 'Or this?' he asked as his breath moved over her like a sultry summer breeze.

Gisele's lower body ached to move forwards to find his. It was like a magnetic field she had inadvertently stepped inside. It was pulling her inexorably towards him. She could sense him there, thick and hard, pulsing with the same longing that was making her heart race and her breathing become shallow and uneven. His feet touched hers, a sexy bump of toes that sent a shockwave of forbidden pleasure right through her body. She felt him then against her belly, the blunt head of him as scorching as a naked flame against her skin.

He worked his way back up towards her mouth, slowly, each brush of his lips setting her skin alight. 'This is what used to keep us both awake, remember?' he said just above her quivering mouth.

Gisele moistened her dry lips, her heart hammering as he slipped a hand beneath the curtain of her hair. The sensations shimmering down her spine made her dizzy with need. She remembered it all. It had never left her. How he made her feel. How he could set her aflame with just a look.

How much she still wanted him.

Time stood still for a heart-stopping pause.

She prepared herself for the press of his mouth; her eyelashes came down, her lips were softly parted, her breath had stilled…

But Emilio suddenly broke the spell by stepping backwards and moving to where he had dropped his bathrobe.

Gisele blinked a couple of times in bewilderment as

she watched him shrug himself into it and tie the cord around his waist, seemingly untouched by what had just transpired between them. How could he leave her like this? Was he doing it deliberately to prove how little he needed her? That she was just another woman he could have sex with if he could be bothered?

He was the *only* person she wanted to be intimate with. She couldn't imagine wanting anyone else the way she wanted him. Her body felt as if it *belonged* to him. It had belonged to him for more than two years.

'I'll give you the rest of the week to settle in,' he said. 'I'll make up some excuse for Marietta for why we're not sharing a room.'

'And after that?' she asked.

His eyes pulsated as they locked with hers. 'I think you know what happens after that,' he said in a gravel-rough, oh-so-sexy tone.

Gisele felt her belly do another crazy little tumble turn but she hid behind her increasingly fragile armour of pride and haughtiness. 'You think two million dollars is going to be enough to make me enjoy being back in your bed?' she asked.

His mouth curled up at the corners in a confident smile as he opened the door to leave. 'I'll make sure of it,' he said and, with a soft click of the lock falling in place, he was gone.

Gisele spent the night in a fitful state of tossing and turning. Emilio's promise had made her so edgy and agitated she hadn't had a hope of sleeping a wink in spite of her pills. Her body had been so uptight with longing she had felt like a tightly coiled spring. She hadn't been able to rid her mind of his aroused naked body so close to hers, *touching* hers. How dared he entice her like that with his mouth and hands, only to step back from her as if she was nothing to him? It made her so angry she had been so close to giving herself to him. It made her absolutely furious to think he knew how weak she still was. He was playing with her, toying with her like an angler with a fish on his line. He was biding his time before he reeled her right in.

She would show him.

She deliberately lingered in her room, taking an extra-long shower, dawdling over her hair and light make-up, determined to keep her distance for as long as she could, hoping he would have long ago eaten breakfast and headed off to work.

She walked down the stairs with an assured smile hovering about her mouth. She would show him how little she needed him. She would keep herself busy all day, sending him the clear message she wasn't waiting around for him to crook his finger and summon her back to his bed.

Marietta was on her way out to the terrace with a tray of fresh rolls and fruit. 'Signor Andreoni is waiting for you,' she said. 'You like tea, *sì*?'

'*Grazie,*' Gisele said, forcing a smile. It looked as if she wasn't going to be able to escape Emilio's disturbing presence after all. It was almost eleven in the morning. He was not one to linger about the villa. He had never taken a day off in the past. He had even worked most weekends, leaving her for long periods on her own.

He was sipping a cup of coffee when Gisele stepped out onto the sun-drenched terrace. He looked fabulously rested, his skin glowing from good health and his eyes clear. He was dressed in black trousers and a white business shirt but it was rolled back over his tanned forearms in a casual manner, making him look even more arrestingly handsome.

He put down his cup and rose to his feet, pulling out a chair for her. '*Cara*, you look like you had a rough night,' he said. 'Your little pills not working, hmm?'

She gave him a gimlet glare as she plonked herself down on the chair. 'Why aren't you at work?' she asked.

'I took the day off to spend it with you,' he said. 'That's what a newly reconciled couple would do, is it not?'

'You shouldn't have bothered,' Gisele said crossly, flicking her napkin across her lap. 'I don't feel like being around you or anyone.'

'Too bad,' he said, picking up his coffee cup again. 'We will be expected to be seen out and about together.' He took a sip of his coffee, looked at the contents frowningly for a moment before looking at her again. 'I have a business function to attend this evening. I thought we could go shopping for you to find something suitable to wear.'

'I can go shopping by myself,' she said, shooting him a look across the table. 'I don't need you to carry my bags.'

Emilio placed his cup back down on its saucer with unnerving precision. 'Gisele,' he addressed her sternly, 'you are walking a very fine line. I am trying to be patient with you but there is only so much leeway I'm prepared to give.'

Gisele saw the steely determination in his dark eyes

and had to look away. 'What did you tell Marietta about me sleeping in the other room?' she asked to fill the heavy silence.

'I told her you have a snoring problem.'

Her eyes flew back to his. *'You what?'*

He gave a little shrug as he brought his cup towards his mouth. 'It's OK, *cara*,' he said. 'Lots of people snore.'

'I don't!' she said, bristling with outrage. 'Why didn't you tell her it was *you* with the problem?'

'Because I'm not the one with cold feet about sharing a bed, that's why,' he said smoothly.

Gisele scowled as she took a roll and tore it into little pieces. 'You could've thought of something a little less demeaning,' she said. 'Snoring sounds so…so unsexy.'

'Are you going to eat any of that roll or just play with it?' Emilio asked.

She pushed the plate with the decimated roll to one side. 'I'm not hungry.'

He challenged her with his narrowed coal-black gaze. 'Are you doing this deliberately to annoy me?' he asked. 'Because, if so, it's working.'

Gisele felt a little frisson race down her spine. She liked the sense of power it gave her to get under his skin. He was still in control but she could see the leash on it was straining. There was a muscle pulsing at the corner of his flattened mouth and his eyes had hardened to chips of black ice.

The air between them seemed to crackle like electricity along a wire.

'You are not leaving this table until you've had something to eat,' he ground out. 'Do you hear me?'

She glared back at him. 'If you want me to eat, then why don't you stop deliberately upsetting me?'

The sound of Marietta's footsteps sounding on the flagstones broke the tense moment.

Emilio sat back and visibly forced himself to relax and Gisele did the same. She sensed the housekeeper's intrigue and wondered how much she had overheard of their heated exchange. How well did Emilio know this new housekeeper? Concetta had been the soul of discretion. Was that why Emilio was so determined that Gisele should occupy his room? Journalists on the hunt for a story paid well for leaks and for photo opportunities. Marietta could exploit the situation if she sensed a lack of harmony between them, and clearly Emilio was fully aware of it.

'Here is your tea, *signorina*,' Marietta said as she placed a teapot beside Gisele, her gaze watchful.

'*Grazie*, Marietta,' Gisele said, trying to smile but not quite managing to pull it off.

'Is everything all right?' Marietta asked, hovering about the table.

'Everything is fine,' Emilio said firmly.

Once the housekeeper had left he raked a hand through his hair. 'I don't mean to upset you, Gisele,' he said. 'This is a difficult time for both of us. There are adjustments and compromises to be made. I want this to work. I really do.'

'Why?' she asked.

He frowned as if she was suddenly speaking a different language, one he couldn't understand. 'Because what we had was good,' he said. 'You can't deny that.'

'I do deny it,' Gisele said. 'What was good about me

having to sign a prenuptial agreement? Where was the trust that most good relationships are built on?'

'I've worked hard for my money,' he said. 'I have the right to protect my interests. If you were so unhappy about it, why didn't you say something at the time?'

Gisele looked away again, embarrassed that she had been so biddable back then. She had felt terribly hurt when he had told her about it but she had kept her feelings well hidden. She had signed the wretched agreement with a heavy heart, wondering if he would ever trust her, or anyone, enough to believe they weren't going to rip him off or betray him in some way.

'Gisele?'

She blew out a breath and set about pouring a cup of tea for herself. 'Can we just forget it?' she asked. 'It's not like we're getting married now. It's irrelevant.'

'It might not be so irrelevant if we do decide to make our reconciliation permanent,' he said.

Gisele's cup rattled against the saucer as she put it back down. 'Are you crazy?' she asked. 'There's no way I would ever agree to marry someone who didn't love me enough to trust me.'

'Love and trust are two different issues,' he said. 'They don't always come hand in hand.'

'Well, they come hand in hand to me,' she said, picking up her cup again and cradling it in her hands.

He studied her with an inscrutable look on his face for what seemed like an endless moment. 'You think I didn't care about you, *cara*?' he asked.

Gisele felt her heart contract. Like a lot of people, he cared about a lot of things but it didn't mean he couldn't imagine life without them. He had lived quite well without her for two whole years. 'Where was that care when you threw me out of your life without giving me the benefit of the doubt?' she asked.

His expression tightened. 'I can do no more than apologise,' he said. 'I was wrong and I have admitted it. What else do you want me to do?'

Love me, Gisele thought. 'Nothing,' she said, lowering her gaze from his. 'There's nothing you can do.'

He reached across the table and took her hand in his. 'Where's your engagement ring?' he asked.

Gisele met his gaze across their joined hands. 'I left it upstairs. It doesn't fit me properly any more. I'm frightened I'm going to lose it.'

He frowned as he stroked where her ring should have been. 'Then we'll have to get it readjusted so it does fit,' he said.

'Why did you keep it?' she asked after an infinitesimal pause.

He released her hand and leaned back in his chair, his face like stone. 'It's worth a lot of money.'

'I know, but you could have sold it,' she said. 'Why didn't you?'

He pushed back from the table and got to his feet. 'I have a call to make,' he said curtly. 'The driver will be here in ten minutes. Don't be late.'

Gisele let out a long breath as she watched him stride across the flagstones and back inside the villa. There were times when she wondered why she had given her heart to such a complex and unreachable man.

'Signor Andreoni asked me to tell you he will meet you for a late lunch,' the driver said when Gisele went out to the waiting car. 'He has some urgent business to see to. He gave me this to give you.' He handed her a credit card and a piece of paper with the details of a restaurant on it.

'Why couldn't he have told me himself?' she asked, feeling annoyed.

The driver shrugged. 'He is a very busy man. He never stops working.'

'I don't need you to drive me,' she said. 'I'm happy to walk.'

'Signor Andreoni insisted on me escorting you.'

'Have the morning off,' Gisele said, placing the credit card and note in her purse.

'But I will get fired if I don't—'

'No, you won't,' she said with determination. 'I'll deal with Signor Andreoni. Ciao.'

Emilio was already waiting at the restaurant when Gisele came in. She hadn't done much shopping, other than pick up a dress and shoes for that evening, but she hadn't used Emilio's card. She refused to be sent off like an overindulged child by a too-busy parent.

She weaved her way through the busy restaurant towards him, conscious of his dark brooding gaze focused solely on her. 'Hello, darling,' she said, offering her cheek for a perfunctory kiss for the sake of onlookers.

Emilio took her face in his hands and planted a hot, drugging kiss on her mouth. Gisele felt her senses spin like a top, round and round and round until she was barely able to stand up. She had to place her hands on his hard chest to steady herself. She stepped back when he released her, sure her face was as red as the single rose in the centre of the table.

'You don't look like you've had a very successful shopping spree,' he said as he seated her.

'I don't like spending other people's money,' she said, throwing him a look over her shoulder. 'If I want to buy clothes then I'll buy them for myself.'

'You seem very determined to disobey my instructions,' he said as he took his own seat opposite her.

'You seem to have trouble accepting that I will not be told what to do,' she tossed back.

He drew in a little breath. 'Careful, *cara*,' he said. 'We are in public now. Keep your claws sheathed until we are alone.'

Gisele had to fight not to glower at him. She picked up the menu and buried her nose in it. 'How did your urgent business go?' she asked.

'Fine.'

A stiff silence passed.

Gisele wondered if his urgent business had been female. A sick feeling opened up in her stomach like a canyon. She hated thinking of him with someone else. For two years she had tried *not* to think about it. Did he have a current mistress he was keeping as backup? Her chest tightened painfully at the thought. So many rich men led double lives. Was he one of them?

'I have something for you,' Emilio said.

Gisele put the menu down again. 'What is it?'

He handed her a jeweller's box, his expression as blank as a sheet of paper. 'I hope it fits.'

She opened the black velvet box and looked down at the staggeringly gorgeous diamond sitting there. It looked frightfully expensive and yet it was much simpler than the one he had given her previously. 'I don't understand…' She looked up at him again. 'I thought you were going to get the old one adjusted?'

'I thought you might like this one instead,' he said. 'But if you don't then you can choose your own. It doesn't matter either way to me.'

Gisele bit her lip as she took the ring out of the box and slid it on her finger. It was a perfect fit and suited her hand so much better than the old one. She had never really liked the previous one but she hadn't had the courage to say so. It had been too heavy and cumbersome for her hand, too flashy, and the claws had caught at the finer fabrics of some of her clothes. This one, with its delicate setting, looked as if it had been designed for her and for her alone. She brought her gaze back to Emilio's. 'It's beautiful,' she said. 'It's the most gorgeous ring I've ever seen.'

He gave a dismissive grunt and picked up his menu. 'What would you like to eat?' he asked.

Gisele looked at him as he flicked through the menu, as a cricket ball of bitterness and hate slowly loosened in her chest. 'Was *this* your urgent business this morning?' she asked, holding up her hand.

He put down the menu and looked at her with a brooding frown. 'Can we get on with the meal or are you still on a hunger strike?' he asked.

'Was it, Emilio?'

'I had several things to see to,' he said, shifting in his chair as if someone had put marbles beneath him. 'That was one of them.'

'It was very thoughtful of you,' she said softly.

'Think nothing of it,' he said, turning another page of the menu with a look of acute boredom on his face. 'It's just a prop, anyway. I didn't want people to talk about why you're not wearing an engagement ring.'

She chewed at her lip as she looked at the sparkling diamond, watching as the light caught at it from a thousand different angles. 'Looks like a pretty expensive prop,' she said.

He closed the menu with a little snap. 'It's just money.'

She met his gaze across the table. 'Do I get to keep it after I've…you know…got through this?' she asked.

'"Got through this"?' he said, with a rueful quirk of his mouth. 'You make it sound like something dreadful you have to endure, like torture or a prison sentence.'

Gisele pursed her lips as she examined the diamond again. 'I don't know…maybe there are some compensations to be had.'

'Well over two million at the last count,' he muttered.

She flicked her gaze back to his. 'So, do I get to keep it?'

'What will you do with it?' he asked with a curl of his lip. 'Sell it or toss it in the nearest fountain like you did the last time?'

Gisele held his mocking gaze for a beat before she picked up her menu. She still couldn't work out why he had taken the time and effort to choose her such an exquisite ring. Was she fooling herself he cared more than he was letting on? She wasn't used to thinking of him being hurt by their break-up because he had been the one to end their relationship. She had thought he had only orchestrated this temporary reunion for the sake of appearances.

But what if he really *did* want a fresh start? What if the new ring was his way of communicating that? Was it crazy of her to look for love where hate had resided for so long?

What if he had only bought the ring to lure her back into his bed? It was way too soon to be jumping to any conclusions over his motivations. She had to tread carefully or risk everything all over again. 'I think I'll keep it as a souvenir,' she said. 'A girl can never have too many diamonds, now, can she?'

His expression hardened all the way to his dark-as-night eyes. 'I'm surprised you didn't keep the old one,' he said. 'The sale of it could have set you up for a year or two at least.'

'I found it much more satisfying to throw it away,' she said. 'It seemed appropriate, given the circumstances.'

His mouth tightened even further as he held her look. 'You're never going to let it go, are you?'

'Is that why you bought the ring?' Gisele asked. 'You thought a little bauble would soften me up enough to occupy your bed once more? You'll have to try harder, Emilio. I'm not that easy for the taking.'

He elevated one dark brow as he ran his smouldering gaze over her indolently. 'That wasn't the message I was getting last night,' he said. 'You were hot for it as soon as I kissed you.'

Gisele felt the heat rise from her neck to pool in her cheeks. She pushed against the table and got to her feet, all of her movements stiff with outrage. 'Excuse me,' she said. 'I need to use the Ladies' room.'

'Don't even think about it,' Emilio said before she had even stalked two paces from the table.

She turned and looked at him haughtily. 'Excuse me?'

'I know how your mind works, Gisele,' he said. 'But running away is not going to help things.'

'I'm not running away,' she said, shooting him a livid glare. 'I'm simply removing myself from your hateful presence.'

His expression became as unmalleable as marble and his voice just as hard and unyielding when he spoke. 'If you walk out of this restaurant without me I will call every contact I have in Europe and tell them not to touch you with a barge pole. The knock-on effect will follow you all the way back to Australia. Can you imagine what the press will make of that?'

Gisele felt the scorch of his glitteringly determined gaze as it warred with hers. It made the backs of her knees tingle with a sensation like pieces of ice chugging through her veins.

Dared she call his bluff?

What if the press dug a little deeper into her private life? Somehow she had managed to keep Lily's birth and death out of the public arena. She couldn't bear having her grief splashed over the press for the world to see.

It was a king hit to her pride to resume her seat but she didn't see what other choice she had. She threw him a look of undiluted venom. 'Happy now?' she asked.

'You've turned into quite a little spitfire, haven't you, *cara*?' he said. 'Taming you is turning out to be quite diverting.'

'Would you like me to sit up and beg while you're at it?' she threw back.

'No,' he said, giving her another smouldering look.

'I'm much more interested in you rolling over and play-ing bed.'

Gisele felt the incendiary heat of his play on words at the very base of her spine. How could he reduce her to such a quivering wreck of need with just a look or a teasing comment? 'You might be in for a disappoint-ment,' she said with deliberate coolness. 'What if I don't live up to your lofty expectations?'

He sat back and surveyed her features at his leisure, pausing for a moment on her mouth before his eyes came back to mesh with hers. 'I'm sure you haven't lost your touch,' he said. 'I still remember what you feel like wrapped around me.'

She gave him a cynical look to disguise the way her insides were coiling with red-hot lust. 'All cats are black in the dark.'

'I've met a few cats in my time,' he said. 'But none purr quite the way you do.'

'I might scratch and bite instead,' she said, crossing her legs to try and control the surge of longing that was rippling through her. 'Or I might just go through the motions to get it over with. Lots of women do.'

His lips curved upwards in a glinting half smile. 'Do you really think I wouldn't be able to tell if you were faking it?'

Gisele shifted her gaze from his, her face flooding with colour all over again. He had known her body so well. Every pulse point, every curve and indentation, every sensual hotspot had been his to tease and please. Her body had sung for hours afterwards. The memory of his touch was still on her skin. It was still *in* her body. She could feel it even now, the on-off pressure of aching need building deep inside her. She would have no hope of holding back her response even if she wanted to for the sake of her pride. Hadn't last night proven that? He had been the one to call a halt, not her. She had been incapable of it. Desire had consumed her common sense. It had always been that way with Emilio. She had no defences against the attraction she felt for him. She suspected he knew how fragile her armour was. How could she keep herself safe from further heartbreak? 'Can we please talk about something else?' she asked, darting a glance either side in case other diners were listening in.

'What are you embarrassed about, *cara*?' Emilio asked. 'That I know your body almost as well as I know my own?'

'You don't know it *now*,' Gisele insisted.

He leaned across and picked up her left hand, bringing it up to his lips as his eyes held hers in a mesmerising trance. 'Then perhaps it is time I reacquainted myself with it, hmm? The sooner the better, don't you think?'

Gisele's whole body shivered as his lips brushed the tips of her fingers. The diamond he had placed on her hand glittered as a reminder of the contract he had drawn up between them: two million dollars for a month of her time. 'Why didn't you do so last night?' she asked. 'You had the opportunity. Why didn't you take it while you had the chance?'

He stroked his thumb across the soft dish of her palm, sending powerful lightninglike sensations all the way up her arm. 'You weren't ready last night,' he said. 'It wouldn't have been fair to take advantage of you when you were tired and overwrought.'

'I might never be ready,' she said with a pert lift of her chin. 'What will you do then?'

His coal-black eyes caressed hers until she wondered if she was going to disappear in their bottomless depths and never come out. 'You'll be ready,' he said with bone-melting conviction. 'Your body is already there—it's just your mind that has to catch up. I'm prepared to wait until it does.'

Gisele pulled her tingling hand out of his. She buried her nose in the menu and chose a dish she had no real appetite for, just so she didn't have to meet Emilio's percipient gaze. It unnerved her how well he could read her. But, even more disturbing, it *touched* her that he hadn't exploited her last night. So many men would have taken advantage of her vulnerability but he hadn't. How was she supposed to hate him if he didn't do hateful things?

'You don't seem to be enjoying that,' Emilio said a little while after their meals had been served. 'Would you like me to order something else for you?'

She put down her fork, which she had been using to push the rich, creamy food around on her plate. 'I'm sorry,' she said. 'I guess I'm just not hungry.'

He looked at her for a long moment, his expression dark and serious. 'Does my presence upset you so much?' he asked.

Gisele made a rueful movement with her lips. 'It's not just you…it's the situation between us. It feels… I don't know… I'm not sure what you want.'

'I want you.'

She felt his statement brush along her spine like a caress. 'Apart from that, I mean.'

'You mean in the long term?'

She ran her tongue over her tinder-dry lips. 'I'm not sure we want the same things now.'

'Isn't it a little early to be worrying about that?' he asked. 'At this point we need to take each day as it comes. We have to try—surely you see that?'

Gisele nailed him with her gaze. 'How much of this is about restoring your good reputation with the public?'

His brows moved together over his eyes. 'Is that what you think this is?' he asked. 'Nothing but a publicity stunt?'

She let out a wobbly breath. 'I don't know… How can I know? You bought me a beautiful ring and yet you've never said anything about your feelings. Not before and not now.'

'What do you want me to say?' he asked. 'You hate me. You've said it several times. What would be the point in me saying what I feel? It's not going to change how you feel, is it?'

She took a breath and dived straight in. 'Did you *ever* love me?'

His expression turned to stone, muscle by muscle. 'I was prepared to marry you, wasn't I?'

Gisele looked at him in disdain. 'So I'm supposed to feel grateful that you selected me from a line-up of hundreds, if not thousands, of potential candidates?'

'Why are you bringing this up now?' he asked.

'I want to know what you felt for me back then,' she said. 'I want to know what foundation our relationship was built on.'

He scraped a hand through his hair. 'It was built on a mutual desire to build a life together. We wanted the same things—children, a solid family base and a secure home life. All the things most people want.'

'Most people want to be loved,' she said with a sigh. 'It's what most people want more than anything.'

'I realise that, Gisele,' he said. 'I would be lying if I said I didn't want it too. I've wanted it all my life but I've learned that it doesn't always happen just because you want it to. It also doesn't last, or at least not in my experience.'

Gisele could sense the conversation was over even before the waiter appeared to clear their plates. Emilio's expression had closed over like a page being turned in a book. She knew it would be pointless pushing him to reveal more of his childhood. She wondered how many people had come and gone in his life to leave him so cynical about love. Had people made promises and not kept them? Said words that had no actions to back them up? Children were so trusting and relied heavily on the adults around them for stability and security. Had *he* grown up feeling he had no one he could truly rely on, no one he could trust to have his best interests at heart?

'Luigi will drive you back to the villa,' Emilio said. 'I have some paperwork to do at my office.'

'So you didn't fire him?' Gisele asked with a sheepish look.

He put a hand to her elbow as he escorted her out of the restaurant. 'He's on notice,' he said.

'Oh, but you mustn't do that,' she said, a frown puckering her brow as she stopped to look up at him. 'He's probably got a family to feed. It was my fault. I wanted to avoid the press. I wanted to melt into the crowd rather than turn up in a flash car and draw attention to myself.'

He smoothed the tiny frown away from her forehead with his finger. 'I don't like it when my orders are disobeyed,' he said, 'especially by members of my staff.'

'Thank God I'm not on the payroll...' She flushed and sank her teeth into her bottom lip. 'Well, maybe I am, now that I come to think about it.'

Emilio brought her chin up. 'You are not a member of my staff.'

'What am I then?' she asked.

His eyes measured her gaze for a long moment. 'Try and rest this afternoon,' he said and brushed a light kiss on her lips. 'Tonight might be a late night.'

Gisele got in the waiting car, but when she turned from adjusting her seat belt Emilio had already gone.

CHAPTER SEVEN

EMILIO watched later that evening as Gisele came down the stairs towards him. She was wearing a simple but elegant fuchsia-pink cocktail dress with a matching chiffon wrap. She had skilfully styled her hair into a smoothly coiffed up-do that gave her a regal air. He had never seen her look more beautiful as she smiled at him, albeit briefly. Her smile was like sunshine breaking through the clouds on a bleak day. He had forgotten how wonderful it made him feel to see it. It was like a spill of warm fluid inside his chest, slowly spreading until all the places inside him were no longer echoing with emptiness.

It was a big step for him, taking her with him tonight. He had thought about going alone, like he usually did. Few people outside the charity knew how deeply he was involved and why. Over the past year or so he had felt the need to stop ignoring where he had come from and do something to help others escape the hell he had escaped. He had done it through sheer grit and determination but he had come to realise others didn't always have the confidence or willpower to do it.

Giving Gisele a glimpse of his former life would be uncomfortable for him but that was the price he had to pay for wanting to make a difference. It wasn't easy facing the dark shadows of his past. He always came away from these things feeling unsettled. He felt as if those ghostly shadows were reaching out of the darkness to drag him back to the gutter and leave him there, cold and shivering and alone.

Emilio took Gisele's hand as she stepped off the last stair and brought it up to his mouth, pressing his lips against the soft skin of her bent knuckles. 'You look stunning,' he said. 'Pink suits you.'

She gave him another fleeting smile. 'Thank you.'

He reached for the jewellery box he had left on the hall table. 'I have something for you to go with your ring.'

Her eyes looked at the box and then up at him with a little frown. 'You shouldn't be spending so much money,' she said.

'I have the right to spoil my fiancée, don't I?' he asked.

He opened the box and she touched a finger to the diamond-and-sapphire necklace glittering there. 'I'm not really your fiancée,' she said. 'It's just a game of pretend to the press.'

'We could make it real,' Emilio said.

Something flickered in her grey-blue gaze before she turned so he could put the necklace about her neck. 'You want the old Gisele back but she's gone, Emilio,' she said. 'You can't get her back, no matter how much money you spend trying.'

Emilio put his hands on her slim shoulders once he had fastened the necklace, breathing in the summery fragrance of her until he felt intoxicated. He felt her skin lift in a shiver beneath his fingers, just as it always used to do. He liked that he still had that effect on her. He liked the way her body instinctively reacted to him, in spite of what she said to the contrary. 'Is the money issue worrying you?' He turned her back to face him. 'The fact that I paid to have you back in my life?'

She gave him a pensive look. 'It's not about the money…not really…'

'What, then?' he asked.

Her eyes dropped from his to study his bow tie. 'You want everything to be as it was,' she said. 'But I'm not sure life comes with a reset button. You can't just pick up where you left off and expect things will be exactly the same as they were before. Things change. People change… *I've* changed.'

Emilio studied her for a moment with an uneasy feeling in his stomach. She said she had changed and she had. She didn't eat. She didn't sleep. She looked pale and frail. He had done that to her. *He* had been the one to change her. How could he change her back? He wanted it all to go away. A fresh start was what they both needed. It was no good looking back. He, of all people, knew that. It didn't change things, brooding about what could have or should have been. Moving forwards was the only way to heal the past. He was living proof of it. Perhaps tonight would help her to see that.

He tipped up her chin again. 'Let's just take it from here and see how it goes, shall we?' he said. 'No promises. Just time to explore what we have now, instead of what we had then, OK?'

She moved her lips in a semblance of a smile but

her eyes looked as if a cloud had passed through them. 'OK,' she said and slipped her hand in his as he led her out to the car.

When they arrived at the luxury hotel where the dinner was being held, Gisele realised the function wasn't actually anything to do with Emilio's architecture business but was rather a fundraising event for a homeless kids' charity he had set up over the past year. She found out through the course of the evening that he had developed a drop-in centre in the city where young people could get a meal and a shower and a bed. His charity also offered educational and vocational schemes to help kids get off and keep off the streets. Counselling services were provided as well as drug and alcohol rehabilitation for those in need.

Gisele spoke to several young people who had benefited from the charity personally. They told her stories of how they had come to be on the streets—desperately sad and heart-wrenching stories of neglect and abuse. It was an unsettling reminder of how little she knew of Emilio's background.

He had told her almost nothing about his past. Had she known him at all back then? Had *he* grown up like some of these young people? Why else had he set up such a charity? What had happened to him on those dark, dangerous streets? What sort of horrendous horrors had he witnessed or experienced? She wondered how he had survived it. How had he overcome such desperate odds to be the successful man he was today?

What had happened in the past year or so that he had decided to do something as big as this? She'd always suspected he deliberately shied away from his past, that he wanted to leave it well behind him. But putting himself out there in such a public way spoke of a deeply moving concern for others less fortunate than himself. It was such a change from the super-successful businessman persona he presented to the world. He was no longer using his wealth to show how far he'd come up in the world; rather he was reaching back down into his dark past to help others climb out of it.

One of the young volunteers, called Romeo, told her how Emilio did a lot of the hands-on work himself on the streets, speaking to kids to help them realise there were other options for them other than crime or prostitution or gang warfare.

'He's not afraid to get his hands dirty,' Romeo said. 'I was one of the first he helped get off the streets. He helped me see a better future for myself. He taught me that you mustn't let what happens to you define you. It's how you handle it that counts. You must be very proud to be his fiancée, *sì*?'

Gisele hoped her smile didn't look too unnatural. She was still feeling so incredibly shocked. The world Emilio came from couldn't be more different from hers. She couldn't imagine how hard it must have been for him to drag himself from such a rough start in life to achieve all that he had. So many obstacles must have stood in his way. How had he overcome them? 'Yes, I am,' she said, 'very proud.'

After a few more words of conversation, Romeo got called away to help with serving food.

Emilio came back over with a drink for her. 'I hope

Romeo wasn't telling tales out of school,' he said. 'He has a tendency to exaggerate.'

'Is this how you grew up?' Gisele asked, looking up at him with a shell-shocked expression. 'Like some of these kids? Why didn't you tell me?'

'Lots of people have it worse than I did,' he said with a dismissive shrug as he took a sip of his drink.

'Why didn't you tell me about your charity?' she asked. 'You've not said a word to me about any of this. In fact, this morning you said this was a business function.'

'Does it matter?' he asked.

'Of course it matters,' she said. 'I thought I'd be forced to speak to stuffy old businessmen and their wives, and instead I'm meeting young people whose lives you've saved from God only knows what.'

'Romeo would have made it without my help,' Emilio said. 'He just needed a leg-up.'

'Who helped you?' Gisele asked. 'Who was your leg-up person?'

His eyes became shuttered. 'Some people need more help than others,' he said.

'So you did it all on your own?' she asked.

He touched her on the elbow to position her to face a man who was approaching them with a camera. 'The official photographer is coming over for a photo for the newsletter,' he said. 'Put on your happy face.'

Gisele schooled her features back into happy fiancée mode as Emilio put his arm around her waist, drawing her into his hard warmth. She felt her skin react to his closeness, to his smell, to the sense of protection he offered. It was hard not to want to get closer, to start to imagine a future where she would always be by his side, helping him help others. He had mentioned they could make their 'engagement' real again, but how could she give him what he wanted most? The one thing he had always been clear on was that he wanted a family, but there was no way she could risk going down that path again.

The evening soon drew to a close. Emilio escorted her out to the waiting car, but he barely spoke on the way back to the villa. He spent most of the short journey staring straight ahead, his eyes blank, the different-coloured lights of the city passing over his features like a special-effects film, making his handsome face take on grimly distorted shadows and angles.

Although he had cleverly evaded answering her question about his background, Gisele wondered if he was thinking of the life he had left behind, the life of poverty and neglect and unspeakable cruelty that lurked on the underbelly of the eternal city. She thought of him as a young teenager out there, huddled under a bush or park bench, cold, hungry, thirsty, terrified, lost and alone. It made her heart ache to think no one had protected him, no one had taught him how to love.

'I think it's amazing what you've done,' she said into the silence.

He frowned and looked at her as if he hadn't realised anyone was sitting beside him. 'Sorry, did you say something?' he asked.

She gave him a soft smile and took one of his hands in hers. 'It must feel good to have made a difference,' she said. 'To think that you're responsible for so many young people getting a chance to live a decent life—

a life they would never have been able to have without your help. It must make you feel very satisfied.'

He rolled his thumb over the diamond on her finger before meshing his gaze with hers. 'In my experience money fixes just about everything,' he said. 'You just need enough of it.'

Gisele felt a little frisson scuttle down her spine at the glittering darkness of his eyes. 'I guess you have to decide which projects are going to be worth pursuing,' she said. 'You wouldn't want to be throwing good money after bad.'

His half smile had a hint of ruthlessness to it. 'I don't take on projects unless I'm sure I'll succeed with them,' he said.

'Success isn't always up to you, though, is it?' she said. 'Other people or circumstances can influence outcomes in spite of what you've planned.'

His bottomless brown eyes moved from hers to slowly gaze at her mouth. She felt her lips tingle and fizz, her heart stepping up its pace as he touched her bottom lip with the pad of his thumb. 'Overcoming obstacles is part of the challenge,' he said, returning his eyes to hers. 'The harder they are, the more satisfying they are when accomplished.'

Gisele felt another shimmery sensation move down her back as the car drew to a halt outside his villa. There was a premonitory weight to the air as he helped her from the car. His fingers as they curled around hers sent livewires of electricity along her arm. She followed him into the villa, all her senses on overdrive as he led her to the *salone*.

'Would you like a nightcap?' he asked.

Gisele sent her tongue out in a quick darting movement to moisten her paper-dry lips. 'Um…I think I might give it a miss,' she said. 'I think I'll go on up to bed.'

'As you wish,' he said, moving to the bar to pour himself a finger of whisky.

She hovered for a moment, not sure why, but unable to tear herself away. She watched as he lifted the glass to his lips, how they rested against the rim and then how his strong throat moved up and down as he swallowed the liquid.

He put the glass down and looked at her. 'Is something wrong?' he asked.

'No… I… It's just I wanted to say thank you for this evening,' she said. 'I had a good time. It was very… revealing.'

He picked up his glass again. 'Don't go out making me out to be a hero, *cara*,' he said grimly. 'I'm anything but. You, of all people, should know that.'

'I think you care much more than you let on,' she said.

He gave a grunt of something that might have passed for mocking laughter. 'Got me all figured out, have you, Gisele?' He took another swallow of his whisky, a generous one this time.

'I think you hide who you really are and what you really feel behind that I-couldn't-give-a-damn façade,' she said. 'I think that deep down you're afraid you're going to get let down so you do everything possible to protect yourself.'

He put the glass down with a crack that sounded like a gunshot. His eyes were blazing with a heat that threatened to consume her. She felt the lick of the flames as he raked her with his gaze, an incendiary heat that ran along her flesh like a river of fire. 'You should've gone to bed while you still had the chance,' he said, moving towards her.

Gisele stood her ground, determined not to be threatened by his devilish and roguish manner. 'You don't scare me, Emilio,' she said. 'You might scare the warlords and the pimps and the drug dealers of the backstreets of Rome, but you don't scare me.'

'Such brave words,' he said, taking a handful of her hair and pulling it free from its restraining clip, unleashing with it a flow of sensations that showered over her like the sparks from exploding fireworks.

Gisele sucked in a much-needed breath. He was so close. He was *too* close. She could feel *him* there: the heat, the hardness, the need that was as hungry as hers. It was pressing against her, calling her body into play. A call she could not resist, even if she wanted to. It was too primal, too overwhelming and way too rampant to be held back any longer.

He tugged her towards him with a roughness that thrilled her as much as it terrified her, pelvis against pelvis, need against need. She could not hide behind her smart comebacks now. Witty words were no defence for the onslaught of feeling that was rushing through her like a tumultuous tide. There was nothing between their bodies now but the desire that had always pulsed and throbbed between them. 'Such brave, foolish words,' he said and then his mouth came down on hers.

Gisele revelled in the fiery heat of his kiss. He took control from the start and refused to relinquish it. He thrust through the seam of her mouth with a bold stroke of his tongue and she whimpered in submission as she gave him total access. He explored her thoroughly, staking his claim, leaving her in no doubt of who was in charge. Teeth and tongues collided, hands groped and grabbed, clothes were unzipped, unbuttoned and at one stage even torn.

'If you don't want this then you'd better tell me now,' Emilio said as he all but slammed her up against the nearest wall.

'I want this,' she said against his mouth, her lips nibbling at his, her hands searching for him, aching to feel him. 'I want this. *I want you.*'

He groaned deeply as she finally found him, her fingers closing around his hot, hard heat, rediscovering the length of him, the strength and power of him. She felt him shudder as he fought for control. He was just as she remembered him: sleek and hard, an intriguing combination of satin and steel.

Somehow she was naked from the waist down; she couldn't remember how it had happened but it didn't matter. There was barely time for him to put on protection before he positioned her and drove into her with a force that sent her head back against the wall, a gasp exploding from her lips as she welcomed him all the way. He grunted with deep male satisfaction and her skin rose in a fine layer of goose bumps as she held him to her. He rocked against her savagely, deep pumping actions that made her body sing with delight, a rapturous melody that struck on chords that had been played in the distant past.

She didn't take long to reach the summit. She only

teetered there for a moment before she lifted off, her body convulsing around his, squeezing, contracting, milking him of his essence in those few blissful seconds where common sense and rational thought had no place, no foothold.

He followed close behind, a shudder going through him that ricocheted through her as she held on to him.

Long seconds passed.

'Sorry,' Emilio said against her neck, still breathing heavily. 'I probably rushed that a bit.'

'No,' she said, sliding her hands over his back and shoulders. 'You don't need to apologise.'

After a moment or two he eased back to look at her. 'You OK?'

Gisele wondered what he was really asking as she looked into the black unreadable pits of his eyes. 'I'm fine,' she said. 'It was…amazing…'

He pushed himself away from the wall, his expression rueful as he dealt with disposing of the condom. 'It wasn't supposed to happen this way,' he said, raking a hand through his hair in a distracted manner. 'I wanted it to be better than a rough grope against a wall. I wanted it to be memorable.'

Gisele stepped forwards and placed a gentle hand on the side of his face, loving the feel of his raspy skin under the softness of her palm. 'It *was* memorable,' she said. Being back in his arms was unforgettable. She knew she would have to live off the memories all over again, but at least she had this time with him.

He studied her for a moment before placing his hand over hers, holding it to his jaw. 'I want you in my bed,' he said. 'I want to wake up in the morning with you beside me.'

How could she say no to him when he made her feel things she'd thought she would never feel again? He might not love her but he wanted her.

He might *never* love her. Some people were just incapable of it and, from what she had picked up about his past, it certainly hinted that he might be one of them, too damaged to open himself to anyone else. It was a heart-wrenching thought but it was something she would have to accept. She could not stay with him permanently without the love she needed, but for now this felt right. She looped her arms around his neck and looked up into his dark eyes. 'Make love to me,' she said softly.

Emilio lifted her and carried her to his bedroom, laying her down as if she was the most precious cargo he had ever had in his possession.

'Emilio…' The soft sound of her voice was like a caress over his skin.

'I'm here, *cara*,' he said, threading his fingers through her hair. 'I'm here.'

'Did you miss me?' she said, looking into his eyes with her grey-blue ones. 'Did you miss doing this with me?'

He pressed a soft-as-air kiss to her mouth. 'I've missed everything about you.'

And he had, desperately. His life had seemed so pointless and empty without her in it. He had worked like a man obsessed over the past two years but none of it had given him any real sense of purpose. He had made money—lots of money; more than he had dreamed possible—but it hadn't filled the gaping hole she had left in his life. The charity helped a bit but it wasn't enough. He wanted more. He wanted her.

He kissed her again, a long drugging kiss that stirred up deeply buried longings that he could no longer ignore. He wanted to feel her convulse around him again in ecstasy, he wanted to feel her grasp hold of him as if he was her only lifeline—the only person on this earth who could make her feel complete.

He peeled back the spaghetti-thin straps of her dress to press a kiss to her bare shoulder. Her skin tasted of summer, an exotic tropical fragrance he had always and only associated with her. He worked his way around to her neck, lingering on the sensitive flesh there, delighting in the way she wriggled beneath him, her soft gasps of pleasure fuelling the raging fire of his need. It was a blistering furnace of want, hot flames leaping beneath his skin, making him aware of her in every cell of his body. She was his nemesis, the completion of him, the missing other half that he had been seeking for most of his life.

'I want you,' he said, pressing a hot kiss to the skin just shy of her earlobe. 'I want you so badly I can't think straight. It's all I can think about. How much I want you back in my arms.' He moved his mouth to the soft temptation of hers.

'I want you too,' she whispered back, her soft lips moving around to play with his in a cat and mouse game that set his senses on overload.

At least he had her desire for him to build on, Emilio thought. It was the one thing he could count on. She might say how much she hated him but her touch and

the press of her lips against his told another story entirely.

He felt the sexy tug of her teeth, the way they pulled
on his lower lip in a tantalising bite that made his spine
tingle. He nipped her back gently, sucking on her lip and
then stroking his tongue over the plump softness until
she whimpered and did the same back. Their tongues
met and mated in a moist duel of wanton need, each one
seeking the other in sensual combat.

Emilio slipped the other strap of her dress off her
shoulder and planted a kiss to the creamy softness of
her skin. She tilted her head, her long hair falling back
over his hand where it rested in the middle of her slender
back. She made a soft noise of acquiescence, a murmur
of want, of need, of red-hot desire, and his blood surged
in response. No one made him feel more of a man than
she did.

He uncovered her breasts and gently cupped one of
them with his hand while his mouth continued to explore hers. She arched up into his palm, her erect nipple
driving into the centre of his palm, her slender hips in-
citing his to press down to meet her feminine softness.
He ached to fill her with his presence but this time he
wanted to take things slowly, to savour each moment.
He stroked his fingers against her folds, delighting in
the scented moistness of her body that told him she
was more than ready for him. But still he took his time,
gently stretching her with a finger, feeling the tight clasp
of her body around him.

'Please...' she begged breathlessly.

'Not yet,' he said against her mouth. 'You know how
much better it is when we both wait.'

She writhed restlessly beneath him, pushing her body up to meet his, her mouth ravenous as it fed off his. He kissed her back with the same intensity while his fingers continued their gentle exploration. He felt her swell beneath his touch, the tight pearl of her need so delicate and yet full of such feminine power.

Her hands began to search for him and when they found him he groaned out loud in pleasure. Her soft fingers stroked along his length at first before she made a sheath with her hand and rubbed him up and down, slowly at first and then with increasing vigour. He felt all his senses roar for release and had to fight not to explode right there and then.

She wriggled some more, grasping the cradle of his hips with her hands, positioning herself beneath him. 'Now,' she said. 'I want you *now.*'

He quickly found another condom and applied it before he positioned himself above her with the bulk of his weight supported by his arms as he surged into her with a deep thrust that drew a gasping breath from her body and a guttural groan of pleasure from his. He felt her body wrap around him, the tight ripples of her flesh massaging him, torturing him, luring him into the deep swirling pool of blessed oblivion. He held himself back from it with an effort; no one challenged his ironclad control more than her. The physical act of sex always became something more with her. It was not just a joining of bodies; it reached him on a level he had not experienced with anyone else. It felt as if each time they made love she reached inside his battered soul with her soft fingers and soothed the torn and ragged edges until they didn't ache any more.

He felt it now, the way she stroked the muscles of his back with her gentle hands, long, smooth, gentle movements that made his flesh turn to gravel with goose bumps. He felt it in the soft but urgent press of her mouth against his, the way her lips were both gentle and insistent, her tongue searching and yet submissive to the driving command of his.

He moved within her, the slide of his flesh in hers slick and sexy, slow and then fast, her body rising to meet each downward movement of his, her legs wrapping around his hips as she urged him towards the edge of rapture.

He caressed her with his fingers to heighten her pleasure. He knew exactly what she needed to take that final plunge into paradise. She was hot and wet and swollen beneath his touch. He kept caressing her, softly and slowly, varying the pressure until he felt her finally give in to the pleasure her body craved. She threw her head back against the pillows and let out a high-pitched cry as her body convulsed around his. He felt every milking movement until he had no choice but to pour himself into her, his body finally collapsing with spent pleasure against hers when he was done.

She continued to stroke his back in the aftermath. He felt those softly padded fingertips move up and down his spine as he eventually got his breathing back under control.

'I'm assuming you're still on the Pill,' he said as he eased himself up on his elbows to look at her. 'Condoms are not always reliable, especially putting them on as haphazardly as I did earlier.'

Her eyes flickered before moving away from his to

concentrate on a point just below his chin. 'I'm sure it's not going to be a problem...'

'Are you currently using contraception?' he asked.

Her gaze met his briefly before skittering away again. 'I'm on a low-dose pill to regulate my cycle,' she said. 'It's been out of whack since...' Her teeth sank into her lip before she continued. 'Since we broke up...'

Emilio felt another dagger-sharp probe of guilt assail him. Gisele had done it tough since he had thrown her out of his life. So much had happened to her: the death of her father and the revelation of her twin sister, all the while juggling the demands of building up her business. No wonder she didn't sleep properly at night. She had said it wasn't his fault but how could it *not* be? Her life would have been completely different if he had stood by her.

He wanted to fix it all, to wipe out all the wrongs, but he sensed it wasn't going to be as simple as that. There was a streak of stubbornness in her that hadn't been there before. He understood how she would want to protect herself from being hurt again, but he wanted to break down her defences so she would come back to him, not because of her need for money, but because she valued him and the future they had planned together more than her pride.

He wanted her as the mother of his children. He couldn't imagine anyone else. He had never considered anyone else. He looked forward to becoming a father. He longed for a family to love and protect. He had dreamed of her swollen with his child. The images had mocked him over the past two years, but now it was something that was just within his grasp if only he could get her to put aside her pride and admit to her own yearnings. She was born to be a mother. She loved anything to do with babies. She just had to trust him enough to let go of the past so they could move forward.

Emilio played with the ends of her silky hair, running it through his fingers, watching as her features relaxed in enjoyment. 'You know how we talked about having a family one day?' he said.

She flinched as if he had slapped her. Then she pulled her hair out of his fingers and, using the flat of her hand against his chest, pushed him away from her. He watched in bemusement as she got off the bed and reached for a wrap, tying it roughly around her middle. 'Was it something I said?' he asked.

'I've changed my mind,' she said, spearing him with a glance. 'I don't want to have children.'

Emilio swung his legs over the bed and reached for his bathrobe, coming over to where she was standing with her arms folded tightly across her body. 'What are you talking about?' he asked. 'You adore children. You own and operate a baby wear shop, for God's sake. You spend hours doing exquisite embroidery and smocking on baby clothes. What do you mean, you've changed your mind?'

She gave him a defensive look. 'I mean exactly what I said. I've changed my mind,' she said. 'People do. I did.'

Emilio looked at her as if she had suddenly turned into someone else. Where was the young woman who spoke so excitedly of having a family? Two years ago she had talked to him about baby names, what sex their children might be, what they would be like, *who* they would look like. They had even talked about her coming off the Pill as soon as the honeymoon was over.

He was thirty-three years old now. He didn't want to leave it much longer before he became a father. He had hoped Gisele would settle back into his life and within a month or two everything would be back to normal. He had planned that once things had settled down between them they would marry and start a family. It was unthinkable to him that she wouldn't fall in with his plans. He hadn't factored in her refusal to give him the family he wanted so desperately. That would be admitting defeat.

Failure.

That word was like a ghost that stalked him. That word haunted him like no other. It was an invisible but all too real enemy from his childhood, the same one that had followed him out of back alley dumpsters in search of food and shelter. It had taunted him; it had tortured him with thoughts of not being good enough, not strong enough, not determined enough to get out of that hellhole. He had fought it off; he had wrestled it to the ground, determining he would never allow it back in his life.

He would not fail.

He would find a way to change Gisele's mind. Whatever it took, however long it took, surely she would change her mind. 'Has this been a recent decision or one you've thought about for a while?' he asked.

'What does it matter when I made the decision?' she said. 'I've made it and I'm not unmaking it.'

'Gisele, you know how much I want a family,' he said. 'You've known that from the start. It's one of the reasons I asked you to marry me. I saw a future with us as parents, building a family unit together.'

'Just because you've made bucket loads of money doesn't mean you can automatically have anything you want,' Gisele said. 'Life isn't like that.'

Emilio tunnelled a hand through his hair. 'Look, I know you got terribly hurt by our break-up. It came out of the blue and shook you badly. Having a child is a big commitment in any relationship, let alone one that caused you so much pain in the past. But we can make it work. We'd make great parents. You'll be a fabulous mother. I just know it. I've always known it.'

She gave him a glittering glare. 'I'm not going to be a breeding machine for you or for any man,' she said.

'For God's sake, Gisele,' he said, frowning heavily. 'When have I ever referred to you as such? I want you to be the mother of my children. That's an honour that I have never asked of any other woman.'

'You'll have to ask someone else to do it because I'm not going to,' she said, shooting him a look that would have felled a lesser man.

Emilio felt his jaw tighten with frustration. How could he make her see reason? Was a month going to be long enough to make her change her mind? Was she doing this just to get under his skin? If so, she couldn't have picked a better weapon. He hadn't told her anything about his past. He had told no one. The loneliness he had felt, not having a proper home and family, not belonging, being constantly hungry, cold and dirty. The shame of not even knowing who his father was. The shame of being an outcast because of the poverty that had been all he had ever known. 'Is this about money?' he asked, barely managing to control his anger. 'You want more money? You want a business deal instead of a proper relationship? Is that what you want?'

Her expression turned bitter. 'That's what we already have, isn't it?'

'That's not what we have and you damn well know it,' he said, frowning at her furiously. 'You made love with me, not because of the money we agreed on, but because you wanted me. It wouldn't have mattered what amount of money I gave you. I don't believe you would have sold yourself. You're not that sort of woman.'

She turned away, her arms still wrapped tightly around her body. 'I don't want to talk about this any more,' she said. 'I'm only here for a month. That's what we agreed on. I haven't signed up for anything else.'

Emilio let out a harsh breath. 'I want a future with you, Gisele, and I want a family. Don't make me choose between one and the other.'

He saw her back and shoulders stiffen. 'I can't give you what you want,' she said.

'Can't or won't?' he asked cynically. 'You want to punish me for how I hurt you. I get that, I really do. I understand that was part of the reason you agreed to come to Italy with me. You saw it as a chance to be as difficult and demanding as you could so I would let you go at the end of the month with no regrets.'

She swung back round to face him, her expression taut with anger. 'And why shouldn't I punish you?' she asked. 'You broke my heart, damn you. I *hate* you for that.'

Emilio put his hands on her shoulders. '*Cara*, if you

truly hated me you would never have shared that bed with me just now,' he said.

'It was just sex,' she said with a worldly toss of her head. 'It's been a while for me. I wanted relief and you provided it.'

'I don't believe it was just sex.'

'Women can do it too, you know,' she said. 'We can separate emotion from sex when we need to.'

'Is that so?' Emilio asked with a curl of his lip.

'Yes,' she said, chin up, eyes defiant.

His hands tightened on her shoulders as he pulled her closer. 'Then if that's the case, you won't mind having sex again just for the heck of it, will you?' And then he brought his mouth down heavily on hers.

Gisele had fully intended to block his kiss by keeping her lips firmly closed, but just one stroke of his tongue had her opening to him with flagrant need. She felt the sexy thrust of his tongue against hers, calling hers into a tango that sent shivers racing up and down her spine. Her body was pressed tightly against his aroused one, the hardened probe of his erection searing her belly with the erotic promise of his potent possession. She returned the heat and fire of his kiss with wanton disregard for her pride or principles. She wanted him with a hunger that was beyond her control. It raced through her veins with breakneck speed, lifting her skin in earthy delight as he tore open her wrap as if it were made of tissue paper. His hands cupped her breasts, his thumbs rubbing over her nipples until they were tight and aching all over again.

He eased the ache with the hot, moist cavern of his mouth, sucking on her until her back was arched in pleasure, her hands clutching his head for support as the fiery sensations tore through her.

Her hands got to work on his bathrobe, pulling it off him while her mouth went back in search of his. She grabbed at him greedily, delighting in the hard sheath of his flesh and the way it throbbed under the caress of her fingers.

He picked her up and carried her to the bed, dropping her in a sexy tangle of limbs, his weight coming down over her, his body spearing hers with a hard thrust that knocked the air right out of her lungs. She heard him give a primitive male grunt of pleasure as her body wrapped around him, a sound that made her shudder all over in delight. He set a furious pace but she was with him all the way. She clawed at the skin on his back, she grabbed his taut buttocks and drove him on with a feral urgency she had no idea she possessed.

It was wicked.

It was racy.

It was thrilling to have him so close to losing control.

She felt the tension in her body rise with every rough surge of his body within hers. She felt her orgasm approach like a speeding train. She couldn't have done anything to stop it if she had tried. It smashed into her, tossing her high in the air, rolling and rolling her in a whirlpool of heady, blissful sensation that surpassed anything she had felt before in his arms.

He came with a stabbing thrust and a shout of pleasure that made her skin shiver. She felt the pulsing of his body as he discharged his essence, anointing her, branding her as his.

He rolled off her and lay with his chest heaving, his

body totally spent and the scent of their coupling fragrant in the air.

Gisele wasn't sure what to say, so said nothing. She
was still struggling to get her breathing under control.
Her body was still tingling from the sensual assault of
unrivalled ecstasy. She wanted to hate him, but how
could she when he made her feel this way? He had dis-
mantled every one of her defences with his hot, drugging kisses and his fiery possession. She squeezed her
legs together and felt the stickiness of him. It was such
a stomach-hollowing reminder of the passion that still
flared between them. Would it ever go away? Would
she be able to walk away once the month was up?

Emilio turned back to her, propping himself on one
elbow as he toyed with the wayward strands of her hair.
'I want you to move into my room,' he said.

Gisele quickly hid a nervous swallow. She had wanted
some space but he clearly wasn't going to be satisfied
unless she was in his arms every night. The intimacy
of it terrified her, not because she didn't want to sleep
with him. She did. It was just that she knew she would
fall in love with him all over again if he got too close.

'What, now?' she asked.

'Not right this minute,' he said, rolling her so she was
lying on top of him. 'I have other plans for you just now.'

'Oh?' she said with a coolness she was nowhere near
feeling. Her body had already betrayed her. It had welcomed him with slick moistness, gripping him so tightly
she could feel the hot, hard length of him filling her
completely. She couldn't just lie there without moving.
She just *had* to feel the delicious sensation of being in
control. She rode him all the way to heaven and back,

finally collapsing over him when she had shattered into a million pieces. She felt him plunge himself deeper and deeper before he let go with a raw groan of ecstasy.

And then, without the need for anything other than the sheltering circle of his arms, she fell soundly asleep...

CHAPTER EIGHT

EMILIO lay awake for long hours, watching Gisele sleep. She was purring softly like a kitten beside him. She had curled up against him, one of her arms thrown across his chest in the way she had used to do. He stroked the silky flesh of her arm, thinking how much he had missed moments like this. She was the first woman he had wanted to spend the entire night with. He had never felt comfortable doing that with any other lover. The physical closeness of sex became something deeper with her. Her natural sensuality was something that had attracted him from the first moment he had met her.

He had loved that she had been a virgin. It was perhaps a little old-fashioned of him to have been so ridiculously pleased, but he admired her for not putting herself out there for just anyone. All the women he had slept with had been experienced. It had stopped him in his tracks to think Gisele had waited until she felt she had met the right man to give herself to.

He had been that right man.

She had waited until she was absolutely sure she was ready for that level of intimacy. He had enjoyed tutoring her. He had always thought there was something highly sacred about her giving herself to him. It wasn't just her body she had given him, but her trust.

It had been such a precious gift, one he had savoured and treasured…until the sex tape scandal had erupted and he had mistakenly believed her virginal status had all been a hoax, a deliberate ploy to gain his confidence in her—an act to put a ring on her finger and a steady income in her bank account. His extensive experience of gold-diggers and social climbers had made his judgement skewed. He had not for a moment considered Gisele had been innocent. That was the thing that still plagued him the most. He had not looked long and hard enough for another explanation. He had gone with the pack on calling her out as little more than a high-priced whore.

It pained him to think of the way he had let her down. Would she ever forgive him? Did the fact that she had let her guard down enough to be intimate with him again mean she was softening towards him? Or had she only done it to ease her conscience about taking the money he had promised her? Was the only thing tying her to him two million dollars? It was a disquieting thought and one he couldn't readily dismiss from his mind.

She moved against him, stretching one leg and then the other before her eyes slowly opened. 'Have I been sleeping?' she asked, struggling to an upright position, her blonde hair all tousled like a bird's nest around her shoulders.

Emilio smiled and brushed a strand of hair out of her eyes. 'Like a baby,' he said.

Something flickered in her eyes before she lowered them, her fingers plucking at the edge of the sheet covering her chest. Her face had taken on a stricken look. He even saw the colour leach out of her face.

Emilio propped himself up on one elbow. 'Are you OK?' he asked.

'Why wouldn't I be OK?' she said, affecting an indifferent tone.

He trailed a gentle finger down the slope of her linen-creased cheek. 'Did I hurt you?' he asked. 'Things got pretty intense there last night.'

She still didn't look at him but her cheeks filled with colour again. 'No, of course not.'

He tipped up her face with a finger beneath her chin. 'Still just sex?' he asked.

'Of course,' she said with a haughty look. 'What else could it be?'

His eyes continued to study her as he outlined the contours of her mouth with the tip of his index finger. 'Liar,' he said. 'It's never been just sex, has it, *cara*?'

She pushed against his chest and rolled away from him, reaching for a bathrobe and tying the ends around her waist, her lips pressed tightly together as if she didn't trust herself to answer. She gave him a final chilly look and stalked across the room.

'Where are you going?' he asked.

'I'm going to take a shower,' she said with a little flash of her gaze. 'Is that OK or should I have asked permission first?'

Emilio frowned at her. He was getting a little tired of her game-playing. One minute she was sobbing with pleasure in his arms and the next she acted as if she couldn't wait for the month to be over. He wanted their relationship to settle down, not be a constant battlefield.

He wanted the past put behind him. It wasn't his way to dwell on things. He had to move forwards. There was no other choice. 'Do what you like,' he said, throwing off the bedcovers as he rose from the bed. 'I'll see you downstairs.'

When Gisele came downstairs Marietta had set out the breakfast things and the morning papers out on the terrace. She sat down and poured herself a cup of tea, but just as she was lifting it to her mouth she saw there an English paper sticking out from beneath the Italian one. She pulled it out and looked at the headline below the main news item. The cup in her hand fell with a loud smashing clatter to the flagstones of the terrace. Her heart jerked, stopped and then started to stutter. Her breathing stalled for so long her head swam.

She heard the firm tread of Emilio's footsteps come out on the terrace. 'Gisele?' he said. 'Are you all right? Have you burnt yourself?'

She pressed the paper to her thumping chest, unable to get a single word out past the sudden constriction of her throat. Her heart was thudding sickeningly, a kick-blow beat that was as painful as it was erratic.

There were two photos. One was of Emilio and her at lunch yesterday. The shot showed her looking crossly at him. It wasn't very flattering to her at all, but that wasn't the worst of it.

The other photo...*oh, dear God*... How had it happened? How had the press sourced a photo of her at her baby's grave? Had someone followed her there the last time she had placed flowers on Lily's grave?

She tried to think through the haze of pain inside her

head. The cemetery had been a little busier than usual that day. Had someone recognised her and cashed in on the opportunity to sell the shot to the press? She knew there were websites where members of the public could sell phone pictures of celebrities: candid shots, catching people off guard with no make-up on or having an intimate argument with a partner—private moments made public for cash. Not that Gisele thought of herself as a celebrity in any shape or form, but re-establishing her connection to Emilio made her an instant target. Was this how life was going to be for the next month? Her still raw, agonising grief splashed over every paper for others to gawk at?

To have her private pain made so public was devastating. She couldn't bear it if her tragic loss was going to be cheap fodder for the press. Lily's short, precious life would be wrapped around someone's fish and chips or vegetable scraps—discounted as yesterday's news.

How on earth would she bear it?

Emilio's dark gaze went to hers. 'What on earth's the matter?' he asked.

She opened and closed her mouth, her lips too dry to make them move. She felt sick. She was *sure* she was going to be sick. Her insides were churning with such anguish and despair she felt as if she was going to drop in a faint. She vainly tried to keep the paper against her chest but her hands were shaking so much she could do nothing but watch in sinking heart-stopping dread as Emilio took it from her.

Time seemed to come to a standstill as he unfolded the newspaper. Even the sound of the paper crackling as he opened it was magnified a thousand million times.

And then she saw as his eyes went to what was printed there. Every word was carved on Gisele's brain like a cruel tattoo: *Andreoni Reconciliation Haunted by Tragic Death of Love Child.*

Gisele saw the flinch of Emilio's dark gaze, the camera shutter flick of shock, surprise and disbelief. Every muscle on his face seemed to freeze for an infinitesimal moment.

There was no movement.

No sound.

She couldn't even hear him breathing.

But then the column of his throat moved up and down, once, twice.

'What?' His one word was a rasping gasp, a choked, strangled sound that contained so much agony it resonated in her trembling body like a loud echo.

She could feel his tension. She could feel every tight band of muscle in his body. His face was ashen. He looked as if he had aged a decade right before her eyes.

She hadn't wanted him to find out like this. She'd wanted to work up to it, to make sure she had a more secure footing with him before she told him what she had gone through.

She slowly released the breath she hadn't even realised she had been holding. 'I was pregnant when I left you two years ago,' she said. 'I didn't find out until a couple of months after I got back to Sydney.'

His throat moved, rose and fell again as if he was trying to swallow something that didn't quite fit inside his oesophagus. 'Pregnant?' he said hollowly.

'Yes…'

The silence was so intense she heard him draw in a

breath. She even heard the sound of his hand against his skin as he dragged it downwards over his face, catching on his stubbly regrowth.

His eyes took on a haunted look. 'You had a baby?'

Her throat tightened over the word. 'Yes…'

He swallowed again. '*My* baby?'

For a moment all she could do was just stare at him as the hurt of his question smashed against her heart like a knockout punch. Then she took a breath and sent him a look that would have stripped wallpaper off a wall. '*How* can you ask that?' she said. *'How can you?'*

His expression contorted with remorse as his hand came back up to rub over his face. 'Sorry, I wasn't thinking,' he said. 'Of course it was mine. Forgive me.' He dropped his hand back by his side. He looked completely floored, dumbstruck, shattered. 'Was it a girl or a boy?'

'A girl,' Gisele said, squeezing back tears.

'What happened to her?' he asked in that same raspy croak.

She let out another painful breath. 'I found out at sixteen weeks there was a problem,' she said. 'I was offered a termination. But I wanted to give her a chance. There was a slim chance she might've made it. I wanted her to make it. I *wanted* it more than anything but she didn't live past a few hours. Six hours, twenty-five minutes and forty-three seconds, to be precise. Not much of a lifespan, is it?'

Emilio felt as if he had been hit with an anvil that had come out of nowhere. He had not seen it coming. Nothing could have prepared him. He stood there in a shell-shocked silence as his thoughts ran riot, each one pointing a finger of blame at him.

Gisele had been pregnant when he had cast her from his life. He had thrown her out on the streets while she had been carrying his child.

A child he would never meet.

A child he would never touch or hold in his arms.

A child he would never know.

What had stolen his child's life from him? What had gone so terribly wrong that she had been advised to terminate the pregnancy?

He thought of his tiny daughter suffering. Had she felt pain? Distress? His gut twisted with anguish. Why hadn't he been told?

'What was the problem?' he asked. 'What happened to her?'

'She had a genetic abnormality,' she said. 'Some of her organs hadn't developed properly. There was nothing they could do to fix it.'

His little daughter had never stood a chance. Would it have been different if he had been there? Could he have saved her? He would have shifted heaven and earth to do so.

Frustration and grief besieged him. He felt the weight of it like a straitjacket made of lead. His emotions—emotions he had never allowed space enough to breathe—were now gasping for air until his throat felt as if it had been scraped raw with rusty razor blades.

'What caused it?' he asked hoarsely.

She looked down at her hands. 'Who knows? The doctors said it was just one of those things but I've always wondered if it was something I did or didn't do…'

Emilio felt another smashing blow of guilt assail him. If it was anyone's fault, wasn't it his? The stress she had been under would have been enough to jeopardise the baby's development.

His baby.

'Why didn't you tell me you were pregnant?' he asked. 'I could have helped you. It might have made all the difference. Did you ever consider that? Why did you keep my own child's existence a secret from me? Surely I had the right to know?'

She gave him a hardened look. 'Have you forgotten your parting words to me?' she asked. 'You said you never wanted to see or hear from me again. I had no reason to suspect you didn't mean it.'

'Did you even try and contact me?' he asked. 'Did you even give me a chance to do the right thing by you and the baby?'

She glared at him, her grey-blue eyes flashing with accusation. 'And have you pressure me to get rid of her because there was something wrong with her?' she said.

Emilio opened and closed his mouth, trying to locate his voice. His chest felt as if someone had landed a heavy blow to it, knocking the air right out of his lungs. How could she think so lowly of him? Didn't she know anything about him? 'Did you really think I would've asked you to do that?' he finally said.

'I wasn't prepared to risk it,' she said. 'You strive for perfection in everything you do. I wasn't sure how you would handle the news of a baby that wasn't perfect in every way, especially since our relationship had ended so bitterly. I thought you'd be better off not knowing. I thought you wouldn't want to know.'

Emilio kept looking at her in bewildered dismay. Did she know him so little that she thought he would not want to give his child every possible chance at life? He would have done anything—*anything* and *everything* within his power. 'What sort of man do you think I am?' he asked. 'Do you really think I would've rejected my own flesh and blood?' *Like my mother did to me.* The words were like a flashback of horror. He blinked to make it go away. 'I would never have done that, Gisele. Never in a million years.'

She bit down on her lip and swung away, her arms going around her body protectively. 'I had enough trouble dealing with everyone else's opinions on what I should do,' she said. 'I didn't think I could cope with your input as well.'

Emilio swallowed against a king tide of regret. 'You should have told me,' he said. 'Damn it, Gisele, do you realise what this is like for me, finding out like this now, and via the press, for God's sake?'

She swung back to face him, her expression full of bitterness. 'So this is all about you, is it, Emilio? What about me? What about what I suffered? You have no right to tell me *how* you feel. As far as I'm concerned, you brought it on yourself.'

Emilio felt his spine tighten with anger. He had never felt so blindingly angry. He was angrier than when he had thought she had betrayed him two years ago. How could she be so cold and callous to deny him the knowledge of his own daughter? 'You did it deliberately, didn't you?' he said. 'You could have told me but you chose not to because you knew that would hurt me far more than anything else. It was your chance to punish me for not believing you. It was a perfect payback. And it worked, goddamn you. You couldn't have thought of a better revenge.'

She gave him a defiant look. 'You always think the worst of me. It's your automatic response, isn't it? Blame first, ask questions later.'

'Were you *ever* going to tell me?'

A flicker of guilt came and went in her gaze. 'I wasn't sure how to bring it up. It's not easy talking about it… about her…'

'You should've told me the day I came to see you at the shop,' he said. 'I came all that way to apologise. I did my best to make it up to you. You should've at least met me halfway.'

She threw him a withering look. 'Some apology that turned out to be,' she said. 'We both know I wouldn't be here now if it hadn't been for the money you offered.'

Emilio ground his teeth until his jaw ached. He felt blindsided by pain and a sense of loss that was unlike anything he had felt before. He was unaccustomed to being bombarded with such deep emotions. Emotions were something *other* people felt. He had cauterised his heart a long, long time ago. He wasn't supposed to feel like this. He'd always made sure he never did.

He had *never* felt so out of control.

How could he ever right the wrongs of the past? Gisele had lost their baby. She had suffered that loss all by herself. He hadn't been there for her. He hadn't protected her or provided for her. He could see now how a simple *sorry and let's try again* wasn't going to cut it. Nothing could make up for that loss. There was nothing he could do to bring their child back. A chasm of pain and bitterness divided him from Gisele now. Was there any bridge that could span that canyon of bitterness? Was there any amount of money or machinations on his part that could fix things? The powerlessness he felt was like being thrown back on the streets all over again. 'I'm sorry,' he said, but his voice sounded nothing like his own. It was hollow and empty, lifeless, soulless.

Dead.

A long pain-ridden silence passed.

'I have some photos,' Gisele said quietly.

Emilio blinked himself back to the moment. 'Of the baby?'

'I brought them with me...' She lowered her gaze from his. 'I have her blanket too. She spent her short life wrapped in it. I would have buried her in it but I didn't want to part with it.'

A spasm of pain gripped Emilio's chest again. 'You have it *with* you?' he asked.

She gave him a defiant look. 'I suppose you'll think it's weird or sick or pathetic of me, but I've never felt ready to let that final link with her go.' Her eyes suddenly filled with tears. 'Do you know what it feels like when people ask you if you have kids? What am I supposed to say? I had one but I lost her?' She choked back a sob. 'I don't even know if I'm supposed to call myself a mother or not...'

Emilio reached for her and enfolded her in his arms, pulling her stiff little body close, resting his chin on the top of her head as he rocked her gently in his arms as she quietly sobbed. He couldn't speak for the roadblock of emotion in his chest. He thought of her holding on to her baby as long as she could. How had she endured such heartbreak? Who had supported her? How could she have juggled the demands of running a small business with the tragedy of carrying a child that had never been given a guarantee of making it? And how cruelly ironic to have been surrounded by constant reminders of what she had lost?

Baby wear.

His stomach plummeted as he thought of all those tiny outfits, all those little vests and booties and bonnets and christening gowns. Could she have chosen a harder way to navigate her way through her loss? Seeing other mothers day after day with their babies. Helping those mothers choose outfits for their little ones. How on earth had she done it? No wonder she hated him. No wonder she had asked for more money. 'No, I don't think it's weird or sick or pathetic,' he said.

She leaned back to look up at him with reddened eyes. 'You…you don't?'

He shook his head, feeling humbled by all she had suffered. His anger seemed so pointless and inappropriate now. Hadn't she suffered enough without making her feel guilty for not contacting him? Besides, there was every chance he might have blocked her attempts to speak to him. His stubbornness had helped him in his business life but he had paid a high price for it in his personal one. 'I think you're still grieving,' he said, blotting a tear as it rolled down her cheek. 'You'll know when it's time to finally say goodbye.'

Her bottom lip started to quiver again. 'My mother… Hilary thinks I'm a basket case,' she said. 'She thinks I'm morbid. But what would she know? She's never lost a baby. She's never even *had* a baby.'

'That's not true,' Emilio said. 'She had you. Not in

a physical sense, but she was the one who stood by you and reared you. She might not have been the best mother in the world, but at least she didn't leave you on some cold, rat-infested doorstep in the middle of winter to fend for yourself when you were less than four years old.'

The silence reverberated with the horror of his words.

Emilio wished he hadn't blurted that out. This wasn't about what he had suffered. This was about her. About her loss. About her devastation. He had put his behind him a long time ago.

'Your mother left you on a *doorstep*?' she asked with wide incredulous eyes.

He stepped away from her. 'You think you're hard done by? I know it's been tough on you, finding out about a long-lost twin. I know it must have been devastating to find out your mother is not really your mother. But she's your mother in every sense that's important. You can't cut her from your life just because you don't share the same genetic make-up. It wasn't her fault. It sounds to me like she did the best she could, given the circumstances.'

She looked at him narrowly. 'Have you been talking to her?'

'No, but I can imagine what she feels like. She's been shut out of her child's life due to circumstances beyond her control. At least her child is still alive and breathing. I don't even know my child's name.'

'I called her Lily,' she said softly.

His throat rose and fell again.

Lily.

'Can I see the photos?' he asked.

She gave a nod. 'I'll go and get them.'

Emilio turned and bent to pick up the shattered remains of Gisele's cup. There was no way the fine china could ever be put together again, which was just like his heart felt right now...

Gisele took the photo album out of her drawer and cradled it against her chest for a moment. Emilio's statement about his childhood had shocked her to the core. She couldn't bear thinking about him as a little boy, cast aside, frightened, alone, vulnerable. How could his mother have done that to him? Who had taken care of him? Had anyone? Was that why he was so closed off and so determined to put the past behind him? He couldn't stomach thinking about his wretched childhood. It was something he wanted to forget. And yet he had set up the charity, throwing himself into the hands-on work with the strength of character she was only now coming to understand.

She put the album back down and took out the soft pink blanket she had so lovingly made for Lily, holding it up to her face for a moment, breathing in that sweet baby smell. She wondered what Emilio had been wrapped in, whether he had ever been loved and cherished even a fraction of the way she had loved and cherished Lily. It was too painful to think he might have never been welcomed, never loved or wanted. How could he have been if he had been left to fend for himself at less than four years old?

When Gisele came back Emilio was standing looking out over the gardens. He turned when she came in, even though she was sure she hadn't made a sound. His eyes went straight to the album she carried. She handed it to him silently, her throat closing over with emotion.

His large hands held the album as if it was the most precious item in the world. She watched as he stroked his fingers over it reverently where she had placed a photo of Lily on the cover inside a pink-and-white embroidered heart. It was a moment she knew she would never forget. He might not have been there for her pregnancy and Lily's birth and all too short life, but he was a father in every sense of the word, meeting his daughter for the very first time. His dark brown eyes melted, a sheen coming over them like the glisten of wet paint. His expression was one of wonder and deep, heart-squeezing emotion. She had never seen him with his guard down. She had never seen such softening of his features, with such raw humanity on show.

He turned the first page and there was the one taken straight after birth, with Lily's tiny body still vernix- and blood-streaked, her minuscule mouth open like a baby bird, but she hadn't had the strength to make much more than one mewling cry.

There was another one after the nurse had washed her. She was wrapped in the pink blanket, looking almost normal. When that photo had been taken Lily had had less than four hours of life left. So little time to say all she needed to say to her. She'd had to pack a lifetime of mothering into a few short hours...

'She looks like you,' Emilio said in a gravel-rough tone.

'I thought she looked like you,' Gisele said.

He met her gaze and her heart contracted when she

saw the glimmer of moisture shining in his eyes. She hadn't expected him to care about a baby he had never known about until now. She hadn't expected him to feel the way she felt when she looked at photos of Lily. She had assumed it was different for men. They didn't have the physical connection with their offspring that mothers did. But it looked as if he was grieving every bit as much as she was. She saw the agony etched on his face.

'She looks like both of us,' he said in a low, deep, pain-filled burr.

She bit the inside of her mouth to keep control of her emotions. 'Yes…'

'Can I…?' He cleared his throat and began again. 'Can I have these copied?'

She nodded. 'Of course.'

'How much did she weigh?' he asked after a long aching silence.

'Just under four pounds. She was like a doll. I could hold her in one hand. See in that picture?' Gisele pointed to the one where Lily's tiny frail body lay in her hand.

He touched the photo, his long finger making their baby look even tinier in comparison. 'She's beautiful,' he said. 'I wish…I wish I'd been able to hold her. To touch her. To smell her. Photos are so one-dimensional.'

Gisele handed him the blanket she had been clutching against her chest. She had never let anyone else touch it before now. 'I can still smell her on this,' she said. 'It's faint but when I close my eyes I can imagine I'm still holding her. I made it for her. She was wrapped in it as soon as she was born. It was the last thing she was wrapped in before she…' She swallowed before she could continue. 'Before I dressed her for the burial.'

He took the blanket and held it up to his face, closing his eyes as he breathed in the lingering trace of their baby's sweet, innocent smell. A mixture of talcum powder and newborn baby, a fragrance so precious Gisele wished she could stop it from ever fading.

She watched as a single tear rolled down Emilio's cheek. She felt for him then in a way she had not felt before. For so long her anger had shut down her feelings for him. How must he feel to have missed out on their baby's short but precious life? She felt dreadful for not telling him now. She had misjudged him, just as he had misjudged her. Would he ever forgive her?

After a long silence he handed the blanket back to her. 'Thank you.'

'Emilio…' Gisele met his tortured gaze. 'I'm sorry I didn't make the effort to tell you. I realise now how wrong that was of me. I should've at least tried.'

His mouth twisted ruefully. 'I probably would've cut you off before you could tell me. I was too proud, too stubborn. I made a bad situation a whole lot worse.' He pulled a hand down over his face again; it made a sound like sandpaper. 'I've handled all of this appallingly. From day one I've been so wrong, so unforgivably blind.'

'We've both made mistakes,' she said softly.

'I don't know how to fix this, any of this,' he said with a haggard look in his eyes. 'For the first time since I was a small child, I find myself totally defeated, powerless. I can't turn any of this around.' He sighed again, a deep serrated sigh that sounded painful as he exhaled. 'You were right, *cara*. Life doesn't come with a reset button.'

Gisele swallowed the lump of emotion clogging her throat. 'I'm so sorry...'

'For what?' he asked, frowning at her. 'What did you do? You're the innocent one in all of this. I was the one in the wrong. None of this would have happened if I'd trusted you.' He walked to the windows and looked out over the gardens, his back a stiff plank of self-recrimination.

'I've been thinking about what you said...' Gisele cradled Lily's blanket close to her chest. 'About if things had been the other way around?'

He turned to look at her, his expression so full of pain it was agonising to witness it. 'Don't try and make excuses for me, Gisele,' he said. 'You would've handled it differently. We both know that. This is my wrongdoing, not yours. I have to live with it. I got it wrong and apologising is not enough. But then, it was never going to be enough, was it? You always knew that.'

Gisele wasn't sure what to say, although she didn't think she could have spoken even if she had known. Her throat had closed over completely, her eyes were burning with more tears and her heart was compressed by the weight of sadness that she had carried for so long. Sharing it with Emilio hadn't halved it; rather it had *doubled* it. She felt his pain as well as her own. She had learned to manage her grief. She had no idea how to manage his. The misery of his childhood had been bad enough; now he had the loss of his child to deal with. It didn't seem fair, but then what in life was fair?

Emilio came over to stand in front of her again. 'I know it's a lot to ask you to stay on in Italy after this,' he said. 'But I will do my utmost to protect you from the media. I can handle the business meetings for you. I can meet with the executives on your behalf. You can stay here, within the privacy and protection of the villa. You don't have to go out in public at all.'

'I'm not sure hiding away is going to solve anything,' Gisele said. 'I'm not sure how the press got hold of that photo, but if they've got that one, they probably have more. I don't want to become a victim and I certainly don't want to be seen as one either.'

'So you're still happy to stay the full month?' he asked.

Gisele studied his expression for a microsecond. She thought about leaving. She thought about packing her bag and walking away, drawing a line under her relationship with him, never to look back. He was giving her permission to do so. Could she do it? But, more to the point, did she *want* to do it? He had, for the first time ever, revealed something about the horror of his childhood. How much more might he tell her if she stayed on the full time? Wouldn't it help her to understand him better? She *wanted* to understand. 'I'll stay on,' she said.

He put his hands on her shoulders, his fingers cupping her gently in an embrace that touched on something deep in her soul. He had touched her in a thousand different ways in the past, but somehow this was different. His charcoal-dark eyes held hers for a long mesmerising moment before he bent his head and briefly but tenderly brushed her mouth with his. 'Thank you,' he said. 'I will do everything in my power to make sure you don't regret it.'

CHAPTER NINE

OVER the next week the meetings Emilio had set up went off brilliantly. Gisele came out of each one with a renewed sense of purpose and vision for her work. It was all happening so fast but she was happy to be swept along with it, as it was just the distraction she needed.

In private, Emilio was tender but distant. She knew he was still coming to terms with the knowledge of being a father to a child he would never meet. She found it hard to reach out to him. Part of the reason was because she was frightened of talking about it in case he brought up the topic of having another child. It was the proverbial elephant in the room. It made her conversations with him stilted. She knew she sounded distant and removed but she couldn't do anything to stop it.

But, in spite of her assiduousness at avoiding the subject, there was a heart-stopping moment when she was confronted with how much Emilio had missed out on by not knowing about her pregnancy and how dearly he still wanted a family of his own. They had been visiting one of the main baby wear outlets in an exclusive department store. Gisele was showing the manager some of her samples and had not realised Emilio had moved to a selection of infant toys farther along. The store manager excused himself to speak to a staff member about something urgent and that was when Gisele's gaze went to where Emilio was standing. He had picked up a soft teddy bear dressed in a pink tutu, his expression so wistful she felt an ache that took her breath away. She bit her lip and turned away, relieved when the manager came back from dealing with his little crisis so she didn't have to deal with her own.

After the first day or two the press's interest in her relationship with Emilio had died down a little, but not enough to make her feel totally at ease. The sense of living under a microscope was petrifying at times. She wondered how big-name celebrities coped with it. And yet Emilio seemed to handle it all in his stride. But then he seemed to know what places the paparazzi frequented, cleverly managing to avoid them. He took Gisele to quiet, off the radar restaurants where the food was magnificent and the wines like nectar. As the days passed, she felt she was gradually getting to know the real Emilio, not the super-successful architect, but the *real* man. The man behind the mask he wore in public. He was making an effort to lower his guard with her, perhaps because he had sensed her closing off from him.

It came home to her in a powerful way when they were walking back from having dinner in one of the less trendy suburbs of Rome. They suddenly came across a young girl who was obviously stoned on some drug. She staggered up to Emilio, teetering on her shabby and scuffed high heels, her skin-tight skirt showing more than was decent of her scarily skinny thighs. She said something lewd in Italian and put a hand out to Emilio's chest. He covered the girl's scabby hand with his and pulled it off his chest, but he still held it within his. He spoke to her like a concerned father would do to a wayward daughter.

Gisele watched in amazement. Although she couldn't understand much of what he had said, she could tell that he hadn't berated the girl. He took her to one side, out of the way of passers-by, chatting to her for a minute or two before he made a call to his homeless kids' hotline. Within a few minutes a van arrived and one of the youth workers came over and escorted the girl into the vehicle, presumably to take her somewhere safe.

Gisele came over to where Emilio was standing watching as the van drove down the street. She looped her arm through his and moved her body close to his. 'You seemed to know her,' she said.

He drew in a ragged breath and released it. 'Yes, her name is Daniela and she's been in and out of our detox programme three times,' he said. 'She wants to beat the cycle but she's got so much going against her—the wrong family, the wrong friends and the wrong beliefs about herself.' He turned and looked at her, his expression haunted. 'I'm terrified I'm going to find her dead in some back alley one day. The police will write her off as just another overdose.' He scraped a hand through his hair and continued. 'Do you know the thing that gets me the most? She could have been *anything* she wanted. She's bright and beautiful but look where she's ended up. How can I stop her from self-destructing? How many young women are out there just like her? Some of them have children. Do you realise that? Who is looking after them while their mothers are out working the streets?'

Gisele swallowed tightly. *He* had been one of those

little children. She knew it, even though he hadn't said anything further about his childhood. She had tried to get him to open up over the past week but he had seemed reluctant to reveal anything else. 'You're doing all you can, Emilio,' she said. 'You're doing more than anyone I know to try and help.'

'It's not enough.' He stalked a few paces away, his hand going back to his hair, making it stick up in disarray. 'Goddamn it, it's not enough.'

She went over to him and hugged him from behind. He was so rigid with frustration, but eventually he softened and turned to face her. His expression looked as if he had come to some sort of definitive decision—a decision he had taken a long time to make. 'I want to show you something,' he said.

'What?' she asked.

He took her hand and led her down a side street and then another and then another. It was a labyrinth of dark alleys and shadows, of scuttling rats and strewn and rotting rubbish. Gisele's skin crawled but she clung onto Emilio's strong hand, somehow feeling safe in a world that she had never visited before. A world she had not even known existed. She felt ashamed that she hadn't made herself more aware. How had she lived for twenty-five years and not have known that life for some people was a daily struggle for basic survival? It made her grievances over the lies she had been told about her origins pale in comparison.

Eventually they came to a back alley that had only one working streetlight. The insipid light it cast was just enough to show the disrepair of the buildings, the neglect that spoke of desperate people in desperate times.

Emilio led her to the front of a run-down building that was abandoned. No lights shone from inside. Graffiti-sprayed slats boarded the windows up. It looked like a soulless body, a shell of something it had once been but would never be again, no matter how much money was thrown at it.

'This is where my mother left me,' he said in a tone-less voice. 'I was a month or two off turning four. I remember it as if it were yesterday.'

Gisele gripped his hand, her throat so tight with emotion she couldn't speak. She let the tears run down her face as she looked at the worn step. She imagined Emilio as a little child, not even of school age. What had he felt to be left here? To watch in bewilderment as his mother walked away, never to return?

'She was a teenager, barely out of childhood herself,' Emilio said into the silence. 'She probably didn't know who my father was. I've heard since there were four or five possible candidates.'

'Oh, Emilio…'

'She told me she would be back.' His hand suddenly gripped Gisele's so tightly she felt her bones protest but she wouldn't have indicated that for all the money in the world. She stood there silently, watching as the memories flashed through his haunted gaze.

'She *promised* me she would be back,' he said. 'I believed her. I waited for her. I waited for her for hours. Maybe it was days. I can't remember now. I just remember the cold. It was so cold.' He gave an involuntary shudder. 'It crept into my bones. Do you know, there are some times when I can still feel it?'

Gisele put her arms around him and held him close,

trying to reach inside him to the little abandoned, be-wildered child he had once been. 'Oh, Emilio,' she said, her voice breaking over a sob. 'I can't bear that you went through that. I can't bear to think of you so alone and so helpless.'

His arms were like steel bands as they wrapped around her. He crushed her to him, his head buried against her neck. She breathed in the essence of him, the pain and the wretchedness, drawing into her being the lost, lonely soul he had hidden from everyone for so long.

After a long moment he set her from him. 'I don't want other kids to go through what I did,' he said. 'I don't want them to spend their lives wondering where their mother went to that night and why she didn't come back—to not know if she's alive or dead. I don't want them to wonder if every man of a certain age they pass on the street is the father they never met.'

'You're such an amazing person, Emilio,' Gisele said, putting a gentle hand to his face. 'I don't think I've ever met a more amazing person.'

'I've never shown anyone this place,' he said gruffly. 'Not even the shelter workers know this is where I came from.'

'Thank you for showing me,' she said. 'It makes me admire you all the more.'

He gave her a twisted look and linked his hand with hers. 'Let's get out of here,' he said. 'This place gives me the creeps.'

Emilio closed the door of the villa when they got home and turned off the exterior lights. 'You go on up to bed, *cara*,' he said. 'I'm going to call the shelter to make sure Daniela is settling in OK.'

'I'll wait for you,' Gisele said.

He brushed the underside of her chin with his finger. 'Wait for me upstairs,' he said. 'I promise I won't be long.'

He watched as she made her way up the stairs; every now and again she turned back to look at him over her shoulder. Her grey-blue eyes were full of the longing he could feel pumping through his own veins.

Telling her about his childhood had felt good. It had felt cathartic. It made him feel as if that part of his life was truly behind him. Gisele had not been repulsed by his wretched background but rather had embraced him with the sort of acceptance he had been hungering for all of his life.

After he made his call he went upstairs and opened the door of the master suite. Gisele had showered and was now wearing his bathrobe. It was way too big for her, almost covering her from neck to ankles, but even so he could tell she was naked beneath it. 'You're wearing my bathrobe,' he said.

'Yes,' she said with a coy smile. 'What are you going to do about it?'

He pushed the door behind him closed. 'I'm going to take it off you.'

Her eyes teased his. 'What if I put up a fight?'

A glint of amusement lit his gaze as he came towards her. 'Then it will be twice the fun.'

She gave a little squeal when he scooped her up in his arms, carrying her caveman style to the bed, where he gently dropped her. He stood back and dispensed with his clothes, watching as her pupils flared as each layer hit the floor. He came back to her and tugged the ties of the bathrobe free, watching as it fell away from her body. He feasted his eyes on her beautiful breasts, the cherry-red nipples already tightly budded. He bent his mouth to each one in turn, tasting her, suckling on her, delighting in her unrestrained response. 'Some fight you're putting up,' he said teasingly.

'Maybe I can't resist you,' she said, toying with the hair on his chest with her soft fingertips. Her hands moved lower, tantalising him with her touch. He sucked in a breath as she closed her fingers around him. How could one woman's touch work such intense magic on him? He wanted her so badly it was like a raging fever in the surging river of his blood. He pressed her back down and came over her with his weight supported by his elbows. 'Am I too heavy for you?' he asked.

'No,' she said, pulling his head down so she could press her mouth to his.

Her tongue danced with his, darting away and then coming back for more. Her lips were impossibly soft, like velvet against his.

He stroked his hands down her body, delighting in the silk of her skin before going to the heart of her womanhood. She was so warm and wet and he was so hard and aching he couldn't resist sinking into her. She gave a little gasp and he immediately stilled. 'Sorry, did I hurt you?' he asked.

'No, it's just you're so big and I'm still a little out of practice…' Her cheeks took on a rosy hue that he found so incredibly endearing.

He went to pull out but she stalled him with her hands on his buttocks. 'No, stay,' she said softly. 'I want you.'

He took it slowly, conscious of her tender muscles accommodating him. She felt so wonderful, so silky and yet so tight. She lifted her hips for each downwards thrust, urging him on, her hands caressing his back and shoulders, her mouth like fire on his. He caressed her breasts, taking his time over each one, his tongue rolling over her nipples, stroking along the highly sensitive undersides where he knew her nerves danced triple time. She writhed with pleasure as he continued his sensual feast on her body, his teeth and tongue working in tandem to bring about maximum excitement for her. She became more and more restless as her need grew, her body rising to meet his as he sank deeper into her. He felt the tension grow in her, the way her thighs gripped him around the waist, her body open to him in wanton abandon as she sought the ultimate in human release.

'Now...' she gasped brokenly against the hot damp skin of his neck. 'Oh, please *now*...'

He played her with his fingers, his touch light but sure. He knew exactly what she needed to go over the edge. He had taught her himself how to relax into the whirlpool, to let it carry her into oblivion. She had been hesitant in the past; she had been almost frightened of the overpowering sensations clamouring in her body, but he had gently coaxed her into embracing what her body craved. Now as he felt every contraction of her body as she orgasmed, the pulses of her flesh triggered his own cataclysmic release. He fell forwards, pumping through those precious few seconds of bliss as her body welcomed him home.

He lay in the quiet aftermath, still with her in the circle of his arms, her silver-blonde hair splayed out on his chest. He heard the rhythmic sound of her breathing, the way on each soft breath out it blew across his chest like a feather dancing ahead of a teasing breeze.

He closed his eyes, sighing deeply as he breathed in the fragrance of her hair and skin, the taste of her, vanilla-sweet on his tongue.

It was the closest he had ever felt that he had finally found somewhere to call home.

CHAPTER TEN

WHEN Gisele woke the next morning she was disappointed to find Emilio wasn't beside her. But as she lay there covered in fine Egyptian cotton, in that richly furnished suite, she thought about why he worked so hard and so tirelessly, why he drove himself day after day after day. Visiting the bleak desolation of that back alley and finding out the true horror of his childhood had finally made her understand why Emilio was so driven and determined. In the past she hadn't fully comprehended his ruthless ambition, but now she saw it for what it was. All the long hours he worked, his single-minded focus on projects that kept him awake at night were not to make him become yet another mega-rich self-indulgent man, but rather a passionate quest to make the world a better place for others less fortunate than him. He wanted to be successful so he could help others escape the life he had once led.

After her shower Gisele went downstairs in search of Emilio but Marietta informed her he was taking a call in the study. 'I have served breakfast in the breakfast room this morning,' the housekeeper added. 'It looks like it is going to rain.'

'*Grazie*, Marietta,' Gisele said and went through to the delightfully appointed east-facing room to wait for him.

With an unnerving sense of déjà vu, she moved to where the newspapers had been laid out on a sideboard close to the table. The Italian paper had a large photograph of Emilio and her coming out of the baby wear department. She remembered the moment so clearly. She had been carrying some of her samples and Emilio had put his arm around her protectively as they came out on the busy street. Someone had been taking a photo with their phone but Gisele had thought they were taking it of a friend standing at the front of the store.

Her heart started to gallop as she picked up the English paper, where the caption was emblazoned there above the very same photo: *A New Baby for Award-winning Architect and his Australian Bride-to-be?*

Gisele went hot and then icily cold. Panic streaked through her. Her heart tripped. Her breath caught. Her hands and fingers tingled as if she was losing her blood pressure.

The elephant wasn't just in the room.

It had escaped. It was everywhere, stalking her. Crowding her, pressuring her to do something she could not do.

'I'm sorry about that,' Emilio said as he came in. 'I was just making sure Daniela had booked into rehab... *Cara?* What's happened?'

Gisele thrust the paper at him. 'I can't do this,' she said. 'I can't live like this. *I can't do this.*'

Emilio glanced at the paper briefly before putting it to one side. 'It's just a bit of speculation,' he said. 'You know the games the journalists play.'

'*Speculation?*' She glared at him. 'Is that what you call it? I call it pressure.'

'*Cara*, no one's pressuring you to do anything.'

'Aren't they?' she asked, starting to pace the floor in agitation. 'What about you and all your talk about having a family? It's what you want. You told me.'

'I do want a family but we'll take things slowly until you get used to the idea of—'

'Stop it!' Gisele put her hands over her ears. 'Don't say it. Don't tell me I'll get used to the idea of having another baby. I don't want to hear it.'

'Gisele, you're overreacting,' he said.

'Don't tell me I'm overreacting!' She felt close to hysteria. She had been in that scary place before and didn't want to go back. She struggled to get her emotions under control. 'I saw you looking at that teddy bear.'

He frowned at her. 'What teddy bear?'

'The pink one with the tutu,' she said, her heart racing so wildly she could feel it knocking against her rib cage. 'In the shop we visited the other day. You picked it up and looked at it. I could *see* it, Emilio. I could see how much you want another baby.'

'*Cara,*' he said soothingly. 'Can we talk about this some other time? You're upset just now. I can understand that. It was a horrible shock to you to see that article. You'll feel different in a few days' time.'

'I *won't* feel different,' she said. 'I'll never feel different. You have to accept that.'

A muscle worked in his jaw. 'Gisele, I'd rather not discuss this with you in this state of mind.'

'I'm not in a state of mind!' she all but screamed at him. 'I can't do it, Emilio. I'm *not* doing it. I'm not going to be speculated on and pressured and cajoled into a relationship I'm not sure I can handle any more.' She stopped pacing, snatched in a scalding breath and added impetuously, 'I want to go home.'

He stood very still, barely a muscle moving, except for that tiny one in his jaw. His eyes gave nothing away; they were onyx-black, fathomless. 'You are free to leave any time you want, Gisele,' he said. 'I am not holding you here by force.'

Gisele swept her tongue over her lips. Her heart gave an extra beat—a sickening thud that reverberated throughout her body like a church bell struck too hard. 'What did you say?'

'If you want to leave, then leave,' he said. 'I'll get Marietta to pack your things while I book you a flight.'

'But…but what about the rest of the month?' she asked. 'What about the money?'

'You've earned every cent,' he said with a slight curl of his lip. 'You owe me nothing.'

Gisele wondered if she'd heard him correctly. Was he really sending her away without a single word of protest? Had all they had shared in the past couple of weeks been reduced to a business deal that had now ended?

What about what they had shared last night?

What about what *he* had shared?

He had let her into the private hell of his childhood. Didn't that mean he cared about her? But how could he truly care about her if he was happy to let her leave? 'But I don't understand…'

'I'll have my legal people contact you with the details of the handover,' he said in his cold and detached businesslike manner that was so at odds with her seesawing emotions. 'You'll own the building and the business outright. You will be able to employ more assistants as things expand. I have engaged a web-designer to help you set up a better online presence. People will be able to order and buy from you online once it's set up.'

Gisele couldn't think beyond the fact he wanted her to go. If he wanted her to stay then why wasn't he saying it? Was it because deep down he wasn't able to forgive her for not telling him about their baby? Had last night brought that home to him afresh? The fact that he had never got the chance to meet his child in the flesh, just like he hadn't met his father? Or was it that he didn't want her in his life any more because he didn't want to be reminded of the pain they had both suffered? Was that it?

No, there was more to it than that, she realised with a sickening jolt.

He didn't love her.

He had never loved her. He was *never* going to love her.

'What about the press?' she asked, clutching at whatever straws she could. 'Won't they make a fuss about… about everything ending like this?'

He gave a careless shrug. 'I'll release a statement saying things didn't work out between us,' he said. 'Don't worry about it. I'll make sure they leave you alone. I'll get Luigi to take you to the airport.'

'So…' She moistened her lips again, trying her best to appear as casual as he was being about it all. 'So, I guess this is goodbye.' Oh, how it hurt to say the word! *Please let this not be goodbye,* she thought. *Don't send me away. Not again. Not like this.*

The shutter was still down over his face, every muscle locked down now. 'Yes,' he said. 'This is goodbye.'

She gave a little nod of assent. What else could she do? She had told him she wanted to go. He had virtually *commanded* her to leave. He had his driver waiting on call. Her bags would be packed within minutes. What was she waiting for? She hadn't wanted to come in the first place. She was only here under sufferance.

Why, then, when she left him standing there, did it feel as if her world had shattered into a thousand pieces all over again?

Three weeks later...

Gisele was hanging some new stock in her shop when Hilary, her mother, came in. Hilary had only been to her shop a couple of times, barely staying long enough to look around. It was the first time Gisele had seen her mother since she had come back from Italy. She had spoken once or twice on the phone to her but the conversation had felt stilted and awkward.

'The shop looks lovely,' Hilary said.

'Thank you.'

There was a little silence.

'You look very thin, Gisele,' Hilary said. 'Are you sure this new expansion's not too much to handle? It's a lot to take on.'

'I can handle it,' Gisele said, hanging another baby jacket on the rack.

Hilary let out a little sigh as she picked up a jacket with a row of baby rabbits stitched around the bottom.

'I know you're still upset and angry,' she said. 'I don't blame you. What your father did was wrong.'

Gisele turned and looked at her. 'What you both did was wrong. You told just as many lies as he did. You *lived* a lie.'

Hilary's eyes suddenly filled with tears as she held the baby jacket against her chest. 'I know, and every day of it I was terrified the truth would come out,' she said. 'I wanted you to know the truth right from when you were little but your father wouldn't hear of it. I didn't trust Nell Baker. I lived in dread that she would turn up and insist on having you back. I guess that's why I was always so distant and stiff with you. I was never sure if I was going to have you snatched out of my arms.'

Gisele had never seen her mother shed tears before. Not a single one. Hilary had always been so stiff upper lip about everything, so stoic, so in control, so emotionally detached. 'I never felt like you really loved me,' Gisele said. 'I never felt like I was good enough for you.'

'Oh, my darling,' Hilary said. 'I loved you so much. I loved all of my babies.'

Gisele frowned. 'Babies? What babies?'

Hilary fondled the tiny jacket in her hands. 'I had four miscarriages in the first couple of years of our marriage. I felt such a failure. Each time my hopes would soar and then it would all be over. I tried so hard not to get attached but I loved each one so very much.'

'Why didn't you tell me?' Gisele gasped. 'Why didn't you tell me when I lost Lily?'

Hilary's lower lip trembled. 'I lost my babies when they were just a few weeks along. You lost a full-term baby. How could I tell you I understood a fraction of what you were going through? I felt ashamed of not being able to be a proper mother. At least you were a mother, even if it was only for a few hours.'

'You *are* a proper mother,' Gisele said, with tears rolling down her face. 'You're the only mother I've got and I love you.'

Hilary's arms gathered her close. 'I love you too, my precious daughter. I love you too.'

Emilio pushed the computer mouse away in frustration and got stiffly to his feet. He stared sightlessly out of his office window. Almost a month had passed since Gisele had left and he still couldn't focus on work or indeed anything. He couldn't remember the last time he had slept more than a couple of hours. He had forgotten the last time he had eaten a full meal. He moved through each day like an automaton.

His life felt empty.

He felt empty.

Even the weather had joined him in his misery. The promising start to spring had been replaced with a capricious sun that had stayed behind brooding clouds for days and days. The drizzle of intermittent rain was a poignant reminder of the aching sadness he felt deep in his soul.

He hadn't cried since he was six years old, when a particularly unfeeling foster carer had told him his mother was never going to come back. He had thought his tear ducts would have dried up from lack of use. But no, they were working all right. He only had to look at the photos of his little daughter for the tears to fall.

He had wanted to do the right thing by Gisele. Seeing

how distressed she was about the thought of having another child with him had made freeing her his only option. It had been the right and most honourable thing to
do. But it hurt so damn much! Was this wrenching pain
never going to go away?

He had received an email from her with a polite thank
you for the help with the expansion of her business. He
had stared at the typed words, looking for a clue between the lines, but there had been nothing. But then
what else had he expected? If she had loved him, she
wouldn't have wanted to leave him. But she had gone
as soon as she had been given the chance.

His secretary, Carla, came in with his afternoon coffee. He didn't even bother turning from the window.
She brought it in every afternoon, even though he never
touched it. It would sit on the desk, forming a skin over
the top as it went cold. 'Leave it on the desk,' he said
tonelessly.

'There's a parcel for you,' Carla said. 'It came by reg-
istered mail. It's marked private.'

Emilio turned and looked at the package she had
placed on his desk next to the cup of coffee. 'Who's it
from?' he asked.

'It's from Signorina Carter,' she said. 'Do you want
me to open it?'

Emilio felt a fist tighten over his heart. 'No,' he said,
raking an unsteady hand through the thickness of his
hair. 'That will be all, Carla. You can have the rest of
the day off.'

'But what about the Venturi Project?' she asked,
frowning at him. 'Don't you have a deadline on that?'

Emilio gave a negligent shrug. 'It'll get done when

it gets done. If they're not happy with that, tell them to get someone else.'

Carla's finely groomed brows rose. *'Sì, signor,'* she said and left with a soft click of the door.

Emilio traced a finger over Gisele's neat handwriting where she had printed his name on the package. It was probably the jewellery he had given her. He'd been expecting her to send it back. He was surprised she hadn't left it behind the day she had left. He could imagine she wouldn't want any physical reminders of their relationship.

The package was securely wrapped with packing tape. He worked at it methodically. He could have used the silver blade of his letter opener but this time he preferred to do it by hand. He wanted to touch where her hands had touched. It was ridiculously sentimental of him, but that just about summed him up these days. He peeled back the tape and opened the cardboard box where a tissue-wrapped parcel lay nestled safely in a bed of Styrofoam cushioning.

His hands shook uncontrollably as he peeled away the tissue wrap to find the pink hand-embroidered blanket his tiny daughter had spent her short life wrapped in. Emotion burned like fire at the back of his throat as he cradled it gently in his hands. He felt as if he were holding his own heart.

There was a single sheet of paper in the box, neatly folded over. He took it out and opened it to read:

You said I would know when I'm finally ready to say goodbye. You were right. Gisele.

Emilio felt a juggernaut of emotion assail him. He hadn't been there at the beginning of their daughter's short life or at the end, but he was to be with her for ever more. Gisele had given him that privilege. How much had it cost her to do so? She had sent him her heart.

A lightning bolt of realisation hit him.

She had sent him her heart.

Mio Dio, what had he done? He had sent her away when all he had ever wanted was to have her close. Why hadn't he told her how he felt? Would it have hurt to have at least said the words? Even if she had still left, it would have been better for him to tell her he loved her. She deserved to know she was the only woman he had ever loved, *could* ever love.

He had been a coward. A pathetic coward, not man enough to own his need for her. Too frightened to feel like that little abandoned boy he had once been, he had kept his feelings locked away. He hadn't even admitted them to himself, let alone to her.

How could he have been so stupid?

So stubborn?

So blind?

He pressed the intercom on his desk. 'Carla? Are you still there?' he asked.

'Sì, signor,' his secretary said. 'I was just tidying my desk.'

'Get me a flight to Sydney,' he said. 'I don't care how much it costs. You can even hire a private jet. Buy one if you have to.'

'Urgent business again, Signor Andreoni?' Carla asked.

'No,' he said. 'This is personal.' *This is my life. This is my love. This is my everything.*

Emilio saw the 'Closed' sign on Gisele's shop as the taxi drew up outside. His heart slipped like a Bentley on black ice. But then he realised it was only seven-thirty in the morning. In his haste to get here he'd forgotten the time difference. He kicked himself for not having phoned first. But he had wanted to see her face to face. He *ached* to see her face to face.

He directed the driver to Gisele's home address and waited with a thudding pulse for the journey to be over. He mentally rehearsed his speech. He had been awake for the entire flight, thinking about what he would say, but in the end he knew he really only had three words to say to her: *I love you.*

The taxi turned the corner into her street and Emilio's stomach nosedived when he saw the 'Sold' sign on her flat.

He stumbled out of the taxi, issuing a brusque order over his shoulder for the driver to wait.

There was no answer when he pressed the doorbell. He peered through gaps in the drawn blinds but there was no sign of her being inside.

'Can I help you?' an older female voice asked.

Emilio swung around to see an elderly lady with a walking frame standing by the letterboxes. 'I'm looking for Gisele Carter,' he said. 'Do you know where she is?'

'She left a little while ago,' the old lady said.

Panic gripped Emilio by the throat. 'Left?'

'Yes, she's taking a holiday before she moves to her new home,' she said. 'She's meeting her mother and her sister in Queensland. A tropical island, I think she said. I can't remember the name of it now.'

Emilio mentally groaned. How many tropical islands were there in Queensland? *Hundreds.* How on earth was he going to track her down? 'When did she leave?' he asked.

'You just missed her,' the old lady said. 'She only left half an hour or so ago.'

'Do you know what airline she was booked on?' Emilio asked as he walked quickly backwards to the waiting taxi. 'It's really important. I need to see her. I'm going to tell her I love her. I'm going to ask her to marry me.'

The old lady smiled as she told him the carrier's name. 'I think I remember now the island,' she said. 'Hamilton Island—yes, that's the one.'

Emilio rushed to the gate lounge after he had cleared Security but it was empty. The illuminated board said the flight was closed.

He was too late.

He scraped a hand through his hair and stumbled to the window overlooking the tarmac. The plane was backing out, preparing its journey down the runway, its lights along the wings flashing in preparation.

A choked-up feeling seized his chest. He couldn't breathe. He planted his hands on the glass in front of him for support.

He was too late.

He rested his head on the window. He *knew* this feeling. It was the same feeling he had on that step. He remembered all too well the feeling of being abandoned, of having no one to turn to, of not knowing what was going to happen next. The uncertainty, the bleakness, the loneliness, the aching emptiness…

'Emilio?'

The skin on the back of his neck prickled. He was imagining it, just like he had imagined his mother's voice, reaching out to him in the dark while he had been sitting on that cold stone step for all of those long, lonely, terrifying hours.

He slowly turned and saw Gisele standing in front of him. She looked pale, wraithlike, just like a ghost. Was his mind playing tricks on him? It must be. He blinked a couple of times but she didn't disappear. 'You sold your flat.' *What an inane thing to say*, he chided himself.

'Yes,' she said. 'I felt it was time to move on.'

He shifted his weight from foot to foot. 'I thought you were on that flight.' *Even more banal.* Why couldn't he just say what he wanted to say?

'My flight isn't for another forty minutes,' she said. 'I'm going to Heron Island. Mum and I are meeting Sienna there. Mum thought it might be a good chance for us all to get to know each other. It leaves from the other gate down there.' She pointed farther down the concourse.

'Oh… I thought you were going to Hamilton Island,' he said. 'Your neighbour said… The board said the flight was closed… I saw it leaving.' He stopped because he was rambling like a tongue-tied lovesick fool.

Gisele rolled her lips together, looking just like a shy, uncertain schoolgirl. 'I was coming back from the rest-room and saw you standing here,' she said. 'I thought I must be imagining things. Why are you here?'

'I wanted to see you,' Emilio said. 'I wanted to thank you for…for giving me our daughter's blanket.'

A shadow passed over her face before she lowered her gaze. 'She was made in Italy,' she said in a tiny whisper-soft voice. 'I thought it was appropriate that a part of her rested there too.'

Emilio felt his emotions rise like a flash flood within him. He had no control over it. His chest ached with the pressure. It was building to a crescendo. He felt every tidemark. They were etched indelibly on his soul. He brushed away the tears that were falling with the back of his hand. 'What if you still need to hold her sometimes?' he asked.

Her bottom lip quivered uncontrollably. 'It's your turn to hold her.'

'She needs both of us to hold her,' he said, gulping back a ragged sob. 'No one can take your place. No one can *ever* take your place. She loves you. *I* love you. I've always loved you. Please come home, *cara*. Come back to me. Come back to us.'

She paused for an infinitesimal moment before she stumbled towards him, a flurry of arms and emotions that he welcomed with every cell of his being. He had never felt so close to another human being. Her arms wrapped around his waist, but he felt them around his heart. *'Il mio prezioso,'* he said. 'My precious one. I thought I had lost you for ever.'

Gisele clutched at him, terrified he would suddenly vaporise, that she would open her eyes and find this was all a dream. Had he really said those wonderful, amazing words? She looked up at him with tears streaming from her eyes. 'Do you really love me?' she asked. 'You're not just saying it?'

He grabbed her hand and pressed it against his thudding heart. 'I love you, *tesore mio*,' he said. 'My life is meaningless without you. I can't imagine how I will cope if you don't say you will marry me. You will, won't you? Marry me, I mean?'

She smiled at him with immeasurable joy. 'Of course I will marry you,' she said. 'I can't think of anything I want more. I love you.'

He crushed her to him again, holding her tightly, as if he never wanted to let her go. 'You are everything to me, *cara*,' he said. 'I am ashamed of how long it has taken me to realise how much you mean to me. How can you ever forgive me for taking so long to come to my senses? How can you ever forgive me for how I misjudged you, which started this crazy affair in the first place?'

'Don't torture yourself any more,' she said. 'We were both victims of circumstances beyond our control.'

Emilio held her from him so he could look into her eyes. 'I was such a fool. I can't believe I got it so wrong. If only I had stopped and thought about who you were as a person, your values, the strength of character you had demonstrated so many times. I ignored all of that. And then, to add insult to injury, I practically forced you back in my life. I wanted to wipe the slate clean but you taught me that it's not always possible. The hurts and blows and mistakes of life are things you sometimes have to carry with you. You can't erase all of them. Those are the very things that make us who we are.'

Gisele stroked his lean cheek with her hand. 'I love who you are,' she said. 'I love everything about you.'

He rested his forehead on hers. '*Cara*, I want you to know that if you can't bear the thought of having another baby, then that is fine. God knows I've got enough on my hands with all the street kids I'm taking in. Daniela has brought in some of her friends. Having you will be enough. More than enough.'

Gisele blinked back fresh tears. 'For all this time I could never imagine going through a pregnancy again,' she said. 'I couldn't bear the thought of going through that terrible loss again. But this time you'll be by my side. I think I could handle just about anything with you standing beside me.'

He cupped her face in his hands, his gaze soft and tender as it held hers. 'And that's exactly where I plan to be for the rest of our lives,' he said. 'By your side, loving you, protecting you and worshipping you with my body and my soul.'

Gisele closed her eyes as his lips sealed hers in a kiss of promise and hope and healing. She wrapped her arms around his waist, leaning into his strength, delighting in the feeling of being loved and cherished.

It was like finally coming home.

Sienna Baker was sitting by the pool on Heron Island, sipping a Manhattan when she got the text message from Gisele. She picked up her phone and, propping her sunglasses on her forehead, squinted against the bright sunlight as she read the words: *Sienna, sorry, slight change of plan. Mum's on her way but I'm off to Italy to prepare for my wedding. PS Will you be my bridesmaid? Gisele X*

* * * * *

Mills & Boon® Hardback

April 2012

ROMANCE

A Deal at the Altar	Lynne Graham
Return of the Moralis Wife	Jacqueline Baird
Gianni's Pride	Kim Lawrence
Undone by his Touch	Annie West
The Legend of de Marco	Abby Green
Stepping out of the Shadows	Robyn Donald
Deserving of his Diamonds?	Melanie Milburne
Girl Behind the Scandalous Reputation	Michelle Conder
Redemption of a Hollywood Starlet	Kimberly Lang
Cracking the Dating Code	Kelly Hunter
The Cattle King's Bride	Margaret Way
Inherited: Expectant Cinderella	Myrna Mackenzie
The Man Who Saw Her Beauty	Michelle Douglas
The Last Real Cowboy	Donna Alward
New York's Finest Rebel	Trish Wylie
The Fiancée Fiasco	Jackie Braun
Sydney Harbour Hospital: Tom's Redemption	Fiona Lowe
Summer With A French Surgeon	Margaret Barker

HISTORICAL

Dangerous Lord, Innocent Governess	Christine Merrill
Captured for the Captain's Pleasure	Ann Lethbridge
Brushed by Scandal	Gail Whitiker
Lord Libertine	Gail Ranstrom

MEDICAL

Georgie's Big Greek Wedding?	Emily Forbes
The Nurse's Not-So-Secret Scandal	Wendy S. Marcus
Dr Right All Along	Joanna Neil
Doctor on Her Doorstep	Annie Claydon

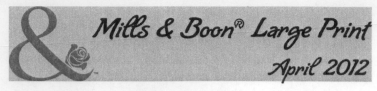

Mills & Boon® Large Print

April 2012

ROMANCE

Jewel in His Crown — Lynne Graham
The Man Every Woman Wants — Miranda Lee
Once a Ferrara Wife... — Sarah Morgan
Not Fit for a King? — Jane Porter
Snowbound with Her Hero — Rebecca Winters
Flirting with Italian — Liz Fielding
Firefighter Under the Mistletoe — Melissa McClone
The Tycoon Who Healed Her Heart — Melissa James

HISTORICAL

The Lady Forfeits — Carole Mortimer
Valiant Soldier, Beautiful Enemy — Diane Gaston
Winning the War Hero's Heart — Mary Nichols
Hostage Bride — Anne Herries

MEDICAL

Breaking Her No-Dates Rule — Emily Forbes
Waking Up With Dr Off-Limits — Amy Andrews
Tempted by Dr Daisy — Caroline Anderson
The Fiancée He Can't Forget — Caroline Anderson
A Cotswold Christmas Bride — Joanna Neil
All She Wants For Christmas — Annie Claydon

0312 GEN STD LP

Mills & Boon® Hardback

May 2012

ROMANCE

A Vow of Obligation	Lynne Graham
Defying Drakon	Carole Mortimer
Playing the Greek's Game	Sharon Kendrick
One Night in Paradise	Maisey Yates
His Majesty's Mistake	Jane Porter
Duty and the Beast	Trish Morey
The Darkest of Secrets	Kate Hewitt
Behind the Castello Doors	Chantelle Shaw
The Morning After The Wedding Before	Anne Oliver
Never Stay Past Midnight	Mira Lyn Kelly
Valtieri's Bride	Caroline Anderson
Taming the Lost Prince	Raye Morgan
The Nanny Who Kissed Her Boss	Barbara McMahon
Falling for Mr Mysterious	Barbara Hannay
One Day to Find a Husband	Shirley Jump
The Last Woman He'd Ever Date	Liz Fielding
Sydney Harbour Hospital: Lexi's Secret	Melanie Milburne
West Wing to Maternity Wing!	Scarlet Wilson

HISTORICAL

Lady Priscilla's Shameful Secret	Christine Merrill
Rake with a Frozen Heart	Marguerite Kaye
Miss Cameron's Fall from Grace	Helen Dickson
Society's Most Scandalous Rake	Isabelle Goddard

MEDICAL

Diamond Ring for the Ice Queen	Lucy Clark
No.1 Dad in Texas	Dianne Drake
The Dangers of Dating Your Boss	Sue MacKay
The Doctor, His Daughter and Me	Leonie Knight

Mills & Boon® Large Print

May 2012